THIS BOOK SUCKS

ALSO BY PIPER CJ

NEW ADULT BOOKS & NOVELLAS

No Other Gods

The Deer and the Dragon

The Fox and the Falcon

The Night and Its Moon

The Night and Its Moon

The Sun and Its Shade

The Gloom Between Stars

The Dawn and Its Light

Accompanying *The Night and Its Moon* Novellas:

A Night Without Whispers

Wing and Arrow

A Year of Tea and Honey

Crown and Crumble

Villains

A Chill in the Flame

MIDDLE GRADE BOOKS

Fern's School for Wayward Fae

The Graveyard Gift

THIS BOOK SUCKS

PIPER CJ

PRINT ISBN 979-8-9854544-6-8

Orders by U.S. trade bookstores, wholesalers,
and all other business inquiries, please connect at pipercj.com

Cover: Helena Elias Illustrated
Editor: Rachel Wharton, Page and Proof
Formatting: Zachary James Novels

*An homage to hundreds of years of vampire media
May we all find an Easter egg to sink our fangs into*

CONTENTS

CHAPTER 1

STOKERED TO MEET YOU

NARYA

He twitched beneath me, a small whimper escaping his lips. My free hand flew to touch him. I ran soothing strokes from his quaffed brown hair down the corded tendon from his ear to his shoulder. He needed to calm down or he'd make this harder on both of us. I relaxed into him, my whole body enveloped by the enormous man in my office.

My tongue flicked, licking the droplets on his neck.

"Please," he whispered. His heartbeat had slowed to a snail's pace.

I ran my hand over his chest, savoring the muscled peck as I found my way to his pulse.

"No," he tried to say.

I pulled away long enough to look him in the eye. He had the bright blue eyes and strong jaw of someone who was good-looking and knew it. His muscled shoulders said he rowed or played lacrosse, or whatever other sport those bratty douchebags who wore Greek letters used to stay in shape. White polo, a yellow E and X stitched where a logo should be, and a small splash of red pooling on the collar. His mouth was made for shouting things like, "Do you know who my father is?" and "Ten no's and a yes is still a yes."

But that's not what he'd said. Not earlier, anyway. In fact, if I remember correctly, the exact words that put him in my crosshairs were, "Have you ever been to Paris? My brother and I would make a spectacular Eiffel Tower out of you."

The cocktail waitress's hand had flexed against the glass so hard I was worried the highball would shatter and she'd hurt herself. It would have been a pity to have blood all over my speakeasy. Well, blood that wasn't my fault.

Katrina Dawn Fournier was her legal name, according to her job application and subsequent W2. She'd been a waitress at a Manhattan bar for two years before switching coasts and relocating to my hidden Seattle gem. I'd definitely hired her because of her skills behind the bar, and not because she nearly shared a name with my long-dead girlfriend. That would be unhealed behavior, and I'm a beacon of mental wellness. Besides, New York was such a cliché, and anyone who agreed with my correct opinion on the metropolis immediately floated to the mile-high application pile. I'd also learned from the paperwork that she was twenty-four, a fire sign, and I memorized her social security number, should I need a new identity.

My name—Narya Volkova—was one of dozens of fake monikers, as people tended to catch on if a successful late-twenties woman doesn't start to get wrinkles or grays after a decade. That, combined with the uptick in missing persons cases wherever I went, encouraged me not to overstay my welcome. The current culture of Botox and facelifts, however, could explain my eternal youth for far longer. And cops only cared about missing people in CBS shows, or if the victim in question was a camera-ready, unproblematic, suburban mother of two.

Men, however… well, they had it coming.

The patrons didn't know I could hear them, of course. How could I? I was across the room with a glass of something that passed for Merlot. I could drink alcohol—drugs and drink were two of the few non-sanguine joys with which my kind could imbibe—but I'd been hungry. The lore on our love for liquor was relatively consistent, primarily as an offering to appease us, but pop culture took its liberations. It was shocking, I know, as Hollywood would *never* take creative freedom with a story.

"Oh, shit," the other man had dropped his voice, brows puckering in apology as he looked at the waitress. He pulled out a money clip and flicked two twenties from the stack. "I'm so sorry about him. We'll get out of your hair."

The waitress looked at the money, then back at the men. "I'll take it," she said, "but consider it penance. I don't want to see him back in here."

She was new, but already holding her own. Ample curves, a pirate's patchwork of tattoos, full lips, and the sort of tan explained by the *Hispanic or Latino* check box on her application—something employers shouldn't be allowed to ask in the first place. She was professional enough to handle herself around rich asshats, and she possessed the strength to emerge from a rough night of dealing with pricks unscathed. A curtain of silken black hair tumbled over her shoulder as she plucked the second man's empty glass from the table.

I already liked her.

The first man made a mockery of the rejection. "Why? *You're* too good for *us?* Listen, princess, when we were in college—"

"Shut the fuck up," the second man said, clapping him on the shoulder.

A regular Cain and Abel, these two, except their brotherhood was contingent on their glory days. Some alumni moved on, others lived in the past. The first one seemed to be frozen in perpetual adolescence, though he'd surely graduated a decade or so prior.

I swirled the crimson liquid in my glass, watching the fumbled attempt at a power play. They were the sort of business assholes for whom I'd built The Page Turner. The ultra-wealthy flies were ensnared in the web of my upscale hotel all the time, as it sat perfectly triangulated between a major bank and the world's foremost tech company. The restaurant and bar beyond my walls were nice—I'd poached the chef from a Michelin-star establishment and modeled the bar after the sort of 1920s steampunk fantasy that ached for the past and longed for the future. You needed a reservation for the library bookshelf to open, revealing the leather couches, rows of books, plush burgundy carpet, and a tasteful, classic art collection worth more than any of these douchebag's investment portfolios.

Men had been mistreating my staff since the 1700s, and though the misogyny evolved with the times, men never changed.

The waitress's stiff smile said, "I hate your fucking guts and hope you die." She tucked the tip into the pocket of her black-on-black fit and returned to her duties.

The Abel left my establishment. The Cain, on the other hand, had followed me to my office when I'd slid my arm over his shoulder, whispered into his ear, and told my appetite it only had to hang on for a moment longer.

"Please," he said again. He was a whimpering puddle of piss and desperation—a far cry from his former bravado.

"I love when men beg." I drained him within an inch of his life before he slumped to the floor. "So, Cain," I said to him, kicking his meaty thigh with the pointed toe of my heel, "what do we do with you?"

It took a three count for him to rally the strength to look up at me. His eyes lolled. His skin had a sickly gray pallor, sweat beading his forehead, drenching his polo. "Don't hurt me."

I crossed to my desk. "Too late."

The Fugio cent rested unceremoniously beside my notebooks, a dark laptop, and my personal collection of books. The coin, also called the Franklin cent, had been one of my first little thefts upon arriving to the land of entitlement and delusion. It retailed for roughly ten thousand dollars, which was all this man's life was worth, if that.

"Heads or tails?" I asked.

He opened and closed his mouth, head bobbing from side to side.

"Come on, Cain," I urged. "If you don't pick, then fate picks for you. Either you live, or you die."

"Live," he mouthed the word, too weak to do much more.

The head—death, as it were—was sunlight, a triangle, and the symbolic afterlife. I tossed the coin into the air and caught it on the back of my hand. I clapped my palm over it and checked his fortune. A ring of chains with the faded words "We are one" printed in the center.

"Tails it is," I grinned. Maybe, once upon a time, this man did have something to live for. A trust fund, a cushy job thanks to Daddy, a line of adoring wannabe influencers who were probably impressed by his party tricks. He'd chosen life. It was a choice he'd soon regret.

I dropped to my knees and looked him in the eye. "When you wake up, who and what you were will be in the past. You'll know only one name: Cain. My faithful servant, my enforcer, my mindless drone. Do you understand?"

His Adam's apple bobbed as he tried to swallow.

I left his mostly dead form on the floor and moved a painting on the adjacent wall to the side to expose my safe. It scanned my thumbprint, revealing a panel that allowed me to punch in a sixteen-digit code. Diamonds, cash, and a tidy stack of passports were the least valuable things in my safe. Six vials of my blood, each drained under the full moon—the only night of the month that imbued my cells with the magic required to keep the liquid from coagulating—waited like quiet, black-red sentinels. I plucked one from the collection and an empty vial in a tiny, sterile bag and returned to Cain.

"First things first, I need a little something for safekeeping." I held the empty vial to his neck and coaxed a little into the glass. *Shit*. I should have done this step sooner. His veins were all dust and hot air at this stage. I had to settle for a few droplets before I moved to step two.

"Drink up, my boy. You're in for a long night."

I lifted the full vial to his lips and tilted it back, watching with satisfaction as its contents disappeared.

A knock at the door pulled my attention away from my now-unconscious monster. He was probably two hundred pounds of muscle, which was no challenge for four hundred years of immortal strength. Unless someone else from the old country had landed in the Pacific Northwest without my knowledge, I was the oldest vampire in Seattle, which made me the strongest. Also the most talented and beautiful, but I digress, beauty was in the eye of my mirror, or however the saying went.

Speaking of mirrors, it was time for step two.

I pulled opened the floor-length mirror on a secret hinge and scanned my print once more. The fire-proof panic room didn't require a code. In an instant, I stashed him in the vault and checked my reflection in the mirror—something vampires can, in fact, do. Bram Stoker wasn't too far off, as the silver mirrors of yesteryear proved a challenge for those of us blessed with thirsty immortality. Silver thwarted vampires and werewolves alike, though it also killed humans if it was pointy enough and stuck between the fourth and fifth rib. Its antimicrobial properties kept the baptismal water from spoiling in the Middle Ages, unlike the barrels of water that frequently left peasants throwing up their guts. The church thought the water killed us because it was holy. They didn't know it was the metal's specific antibacterial properties that fought the contagion coursing through our veins.

So, for hundreds of years, if I wanted to see my striking gray eyes or spectacular tits, I'd have to look into a puddle at nighttime by candlelight. Such a pity. Dracula would have loved looking into the modern glass and aluminum. I was unruffled, saved for a dribble of blood that I rubbed into the rouge of my lipstick.

I opened the door to my office, lips twitching in a smile.

"Hey, Katrina," I said. "How's the night treating you?"

She looked over my shoulder. "I go by Kit," she corrected me. "I saw that guy come back here with you and wanted to make sure you were okay."

I nearly choked. This fragile, mortal thing wanted to make sure *I* was okay?

"I just didn't like the idea of a guy like that..." Her gaze dropped to her shoes as if embarrassed that she'd bothered.

My hand flicked out and landed on her arm. I couldn't help it, I gave in to the urge to run it along her warm skin, from her elbow to her shoulder. I gave her a light squeeze. "That was very thoughtful of you. I'm fine. How are you? Did they bother you?"

Her dark eyes peered into mine. Something inside me squeezed. My eyes flicked to her throat, but not for the blood. Her full lips, the flush of her cheeks, her heavy lashes...fuck, it required more self-control not to pull her into my office and pin her against the wall than it had to keep myself from murdering the frat boy.

Stop it, my conscience scolded. *You won't make it to a thousand if you're reckless, and it would be a tragedy for you to die young.*

"All men bother me," she said, smile wry.

Hope fluttered in my stomach. "Are you gay?"

Are you kidding me? The voice practically screamed. *Why would you say that? You can't ask that of your employees.*

"Oh, uh." Kit's nose wrinkled. "Um. I'm queer. I'm bi, I guess? I haven't had a… I mean, I'm pan, maybe? But I have a… I… is it…"

I brushed it aside as quickly as I could, gesturing with forced casualness to the ornate arrangement of dried flowers on my desk. The gradient of orange, white, and pink denoted my proclivities. "The Page Turner is an LGBTQ+ friendly establishment," I said as smoothly as I could. I didn't understand the single butterfly—moth, perhaps—that she'd mentioned her queerness at all. I was with the times. I wasn't stuck in the ass-pinching 50s when women were afraid of reporting their inappropriate bosses to HR.

She was a human. She was a cocktail waitress at my bar. She was off limits.

Besides, her name was Katrina, not Cetina. As if that would have been some divine reincarnation from the universe, if I believed in signs.

It was at that moment I realized I was still touching her. My hand dropped. My shoulders straightened. "Would you like to come in? Discuss your second week on the job, perhaps?"

"No, I…oh! Boss, you have—" her hand lifted as if to touch my face. The resurgence of moths filled me as I ached for her to close the final inch. The moment she touched me, my hand would close over hers. I'd guide her into the office, and close the door behind her. I'd be able to taste the sharp inhale of her surprise as my tongue explored her mouth, hands on her hips, her back, her ass, tangled in her hair.

When her hand dropped to her black pants and plucked a silk kerchief monogrammed with the speakeasy's logo, I understood what she was saying. My eagle-sharp vision caught my reflection in her dark eyes. A single drop of blood dripped from the corner of my mouth.

I lifted my thumb to catch the drop before it made it to my chin, locking eyes with Kit. Her mouth opened, eyes widening as my thumb slowly pushed the drop upward over my lower lip, sucking it clean.

I caught the uptick in her pulse as she watched, and couldn't help but smile.

Oh, yes. I liked this one.

Dear Cetina,

Do you remember that woman I told you about? The one who shared your dark hair, and enough vowels and consonants of your name to convince me that her resume should go to the top of the pile? She's nice. You wouldn't date her, of course. You like your women cunty, which is the only reason I got a shot.

You'd love my new henchman, however. He was the sort we used to love to swindle. Remember Count Litovoi? He insisted he was a prince of Wallachia and would "pay us back later". Amazing. Men never change. It's comforting, in a way, in a world that I hardly recognize, to have a constant.

I'm making them pay, every day, for what they did to you.

With all my love, forever,
Yours

CHAPTER 2

SOMETHING NEW TO HEAT MY BLOOD

KIT

None of the songs were quite right as I drove home. The January drizzle and the windshield wiper's rhythmic answer matched the rain's relentless music. I was looking for a throb, a pulse, a heat to match the confusion that had stamped my face in a permanent blush, blooming in a new and different heat between my legs.

I loved clapping back at trust fund babies, but never before had it resulted in...*this*.

I found street parking on a shadowed incline. The street was silent at three in the morning, but I knew my boyfriend would be awake. I sat in the car rallying the courage to go inside. He wasn't violent. At least, not in the conventional sense. But I'd been in fight-or-flight over the verbal and emotional abuse for the last six months. His manipulative ass knew when to shower sweetness whenever he sensed I'd almost mustered the courage to bolt. The rest of our relationship was one behavior-modifying punishment after the next. I was so tired that I wondered if I stayed just to catch the rare moments of peace when he was the kind, funny Adonis that he'd tricked me into thinking he was when we'd first started dating. He loved to complain about how hard he worked and his insane hours, but most of his stress could be attributed to poor time management and the hours-long breaks for PC gaming. At least if he was awake, I'd be able to see if he could help me with the need pumping between my thighs. Sex was one of the few things we did right.

"Hey, babe," he said, not looking up from the screen as I entered his apartment. His thumbs moved quickly across the controller attachment. The sounds of hacking and slashing tore from his side-scroller. "How was work?"

I tossed my keys on the counter. "Wanna fuck?"

His eyes flashed from the screen to me. His lips twitched. "You're not gonna try to buy me dinner first?"

"Come on, Andy," I urged, "turn off the game. Get in the shower with me before bed."

He looked frustrated that my talking had forced him to press pause. "I still have another hour of work at least."

I kept myself from sarcastically repeating the word. He blamed me for picking fights whenever I attempted to engage in any version of reality that didn't match his own. "Okay," I said, "quick break, then? Let me suck your dick in the shower while I wash off six hours of sweat, and then you can finish your…work."

I could see from his flattened expression that I'd fucked up. He tasted the insincerity on my words.

"I'm just taking a break, Kit. I need my brain fresh. Cryptocurrency is the future, you know? I'm literally shaping the evolution of humanity. I *am* working."

"I know, I know," I raised my hands to soothe him. "I'm sorry. I'll shower and then see if you're in the mood when I get out?"

He set down the controller a little too loudly. "Why are you pushing it when I already told you I have work? It's not sexy when you try to force it on me, and if I'm being honest, it's not very feminist of you."

"I'm sorry," I said. "Should I go sleep at mine tonight?"

He looked like I'd slapped him. "You pick a fight, and just because I won't give you what you want, you storm out? Why are you like this?"

The heat I'd felt moments prior turned to ice. Cortisol filled my body, stomach rolling against the nausea. "I'm sorry, Andy. I wasn't trying to fight."

I waited to talk it out, but he turned back to his game, happy to ignore me. I stood for nearly a minute, listening to the lights and sounds that he deemed more important than his girlfriend. He muttered something sarcastic about having a good shower, I couldn't quite hear him as I closed and locked the bathroom door behind me. I would have driven home if it didn't take me thirty minutes to get there. Besides, he iced me out for several days any time I left. The panic attacks I'd get in the Arctic silence kept me coming back, promising I wouldn't pick fights again. I was better off staying in the hostile territory of his tech-bro apartment if I wanted to reestablish peace. As an aside, my apartment was neither for me nor for sleeping. I'd only held onto it to facilitate the in-calls for my side hustle.

Andy had claimed it was hot, that it was sexually self-actualized; that I was a modern woman when I'd told him I escorted a few times per month. It had been empowering music to my ears at the time. Now, he loved to throw it in my face whenever he needed to feel superior. I continued seeing clients and he knew it, but to keep the peace, I stopped talking about it.

How was I to know he was such a goddamn liar?

I was a grown woman. I had no idea how I'd gotten myself into a fucked up relationship with a narcissist. He'd been my goddamn prince charming when we'd first met. He opened the doors, picked up the bills, made me cum like a fountain, brought me coffee in bed, and every day, asked how he could make my life a little better. I was so fucking happy, and such a goddamn idiot.

I'd never been love-bombed before him.

And honestly, none of it was suspicious. He was right to be obsessed with me. I made my own money, was quick-witted and well-read, and looked great naked. I'd just moved here from New York and didn't have a support system to tell me that he was a bouquet of red flags. Now I was in over my head.

I fished the waterproof dildo from my side of the sink and turned on the water in the shower.

The hot water felt amazing. Every drop washed off rich pricks and narcissists and hours of capitalism. I lathered with shampoo, thinking of another's fingers in my hair. I pictured soft, feminine hands sudsing soap over my arms, my stomach, my legs, my breasts.

Suddenly, I was daydreaming about my boss's face, her manicured hands, her cherry-dark lips, her razor-sharp cat eye and smoldering pale gaze. I wasn't used to that kind of attention. Not from someone like her. It wasn't like I was inexperienced. I'd fumbled my way around a woman's body as the sexual prop in clients' threesomes before. But being one-on-one with someone like Narya was...different. She carried herself like she knew something the rest of us didn't; like she was in on a joke that was just out of earshot. She seemed to own an infinite supply of scandalously plunging silk tops, and if she owned a bra, I'd never seen evidence of it. Her name had to be Eastern European, and while I'd heard of beautiful women coming from Baltic countries and Russia, beautiful was not a drastic enough superlative for how fucking stunning she was.

When my memory drifted to her thumb catching the cut on her lip, I brought the dildo to my chin, tracing it up to my lips, just as her finger had traced that drop. I eased it into my mouth, thinking of that thumb, then sucked lightly, just as she had done.

I closed my eyes and turned it on, feeling the vibrations on my mouth, down the front of my throat, down my center, and then teased my southernmost lips just around the entrance. Andy may as well not have existed. He certainly wasn't the one on my mind when I slipped it inside.

Journal—

What the fuck? I mean seriously, what the fuck?

Why am I with this man who isn't even nice to me? For a while, I told myself that it was fine to stay for great sex, but he won't even fuck me anymore unless it's on his terms.

Maybe that's why I started writing in you again. I needed to be able to look back on these pages to remind myself of who he is and how he makes me feel on those days I'm surviving on the breadcrumbs that masquerade as the bare minimum. The tiny highs aren't cutting it anymore. So why am I still here?

And tell me why I still men give a shot when I've never met one who didn't let me down? I'm a bad bisexual. Pansexual. Whatever I am. Especially when there are women who...well, okay, I don't know if she's interested in me. But she's incredible. I can't say I usually think of women when I touch myself, but fuck if I didn't have a fireworks orgasm in the shower just now thinking about this exchange Narya and I had at work. I mean, she's my boss, but...it was so fucking sexy. And if she did like me like that... Honestly, never mind. Now that I've written it down, I see how insane it sounds. She's a hard dime. She's utterly stunning in one of those unapproachable supermodel ways, but manages to surprise you with these incredible moments of levity or humanity. She's so accomplished. I mean, this woman has her shit <u>together</u>. Meanwhile, I barely remember to take my birth control or where I left my keys.

They're always in the key bowl. Always! So why do I search everywhere else, first?

Maybe that's why I need to write things down to process them. I'm a space case.

Anyway, the job is okay.

Life is...okay.

I'm not sure if it ever gets better, despite what the PSAs say. Not with Andy, anyway.

Maybe that's okay.

Maybe it's not.

Either way, it's what it is.

Tired,
Kit

CHAPTER 3

True Blood(lust)

Narya

The night was dragging.

I didn't want to admit to myself that I was waiting for Kit's shift to start, but damn, was the clock frozen?

A slow parade of people filtered in and out of the bar. Humans, with their voracious need for entertainment, flitted from table to table like bees seeking nectar. The ambrosia of choice here was top-shelf booze, dim lights, and an illusion of exclusivity. The kind of place that made them think they were part of something special.

The entertainment, well…there was a reason I'd chosen to put my speakeasy in a hotel.

I watched a mediocre man seal the deal with someone so far out of his league that I was curious how she could even see such an ant from her place atop Everest. Straight women and their tolerance for male mediocrity was truly something.

If he couldn't seal the deal himself, I could help.

Not with her. God, no. That poor girl wasn't being compensated for the horror of tolerating Jeff the stockbroker and his painfully pinched features. I made eye contact with one of my butterflies—that's what I called them, anyway—and she chuckled at Jeff and the goddess who may as well have been Cleopatra. The butterfly gave me a subtle toast with her drink, and I shrugged in return. We'd picked him out at the start of her shift as a potential John, but it was of no bother. Dick was plentiful and low in value.

Pussy, on the other hand...

Well, for anyone to understand my bar, my butterflies, any of it, really, I'd need to be willing to talk about the gruesome way I was changed into what I am today. I'd never tell it, of course. A thousand years could pass and I'd still curl with white-hot fury whenever I thought about my life in the brothel back when Romania still belonged to the Ottoman Empire. I thought about the sisterhood I'd forged with the other women, the love I'd found in Cetina, the relief of having a roof over my head and food in my belly, and the happy faces on deeply pleased patrons.

I wouldn't let myself think of the man who'd entered a home of fifty, and left only one alive.

Was "alive" the right word? It didn't seem to apply to me.

His appetite for blood hadn't stopped at his stomach. He'd claimed he was a descendant of Vlad the Impaler, and after what he'd done to my sisters and the men in their beds, I'd have to agree. I'd only been allowed to live because of the words I'd screamed when he'd raised his scythe above his head, ready to let my empty expression join the dismembered pile of corpses and lake of blood.

"I'll meet you in heaven," I'd cried, clutching what remained of the woman I'd loved. I then snarled at him and said, "But you —you'll burn in Hell."

He'd lowered his scythe and smiled a slow, horrible smile. "Oh, I can ensure you'll never be reunited with your precious Cetina. Not even in the afterlife."

He was right.

I'd hunted him to a lavish mansion in Stockholm in the early 1800s, and it took me fifty days of plucking him apart to avenge those fifty lives, one excruciating piece at a time.

Hundreds of years later, I became den mother to my fiercely protected butterflies. We were no longer a brothel, but an upscale hotel. Every visit was monitored, and I could descend upon any room with ferocious and instantaneous justice, should I need.

I wasn't worried about dying. I mean, media had gotten a few things right about ways to kill us. Garlic, holy water, and crosses were the sort of thing that many of us pretended would have worked for a few centuries, if only because it was nice to give humans a false sense of protection. It kept them from picking up pitchforks and burning innocent men and women, which was important to the bloodsuckers among us who cared about innocents. And for those of us who didn't, it made our food source more vulnerable when they had a placebo to keep them warm at night.

A stake through the heart? Beheading? They both work impeccably, but then again, name a creature—supernatural or mortal alike—who would survive that shit. If a man's first instinct was to take out his hacksaw and behead me before I could rip his arm off, then he'd fairly bested me in battle. That said, men were usually too busy screaming to intelligently react, and vampire hunters were pretty limited to the classic Van Helsing or the modern Winchester or Buffy. Humans were too obsessed with their self-assigned role as apex predators to actually fear the things in the shadows. The only thing we needed to protect us was their unwillingness to believe.

I watched the bookcase open, smiling at the obedient henchman who closed it behind Jeff and his conquest. Cain loomed near the door, arms crossed, his face a perfect mask of indifference. I could practically see the single brain cell bouncing around in his skull like a ping-pong ball. He stood too stiffly, like he wasn't sure if he was supposed to guard the door, glare at customers, or salute me every time I walked by.

He'd been difficult to break in, even with my blood coursing through his veins. A frat boy, through and through—those types were always the worst. Clinging to whatever vestiges of their former "glory days" they could muster. It was almost impressive how consistently disappointing he managed to be. Almost.

One of the bartenders, Jensen, shot Cain a look of bewilderment as he passed, then turned his confusion toward me. "What's he doing here?" Jensen mouthed, jerking his head towards Cain.

I let out a dramatic sigh, feigning exasperation for Jensen's benefit. "I told him he could either get out of my club forever or take a job and prove he wasn't just another waste of space," I said, loud enough for Cain to hear. He didn't react, his eyes focused on a point just over my head. "Turns out, his father owns a security company. Lucky for us, we could use a bouncer. Plus," I shrugged, the picture of nonchalance, "it's fun watching him try to look useful."

Jensen stifled his smile, nodding as he bused another tray of empty drinks and returned to the bar. I wasn't lying. We needed better security, and Cain wasn't entirely useless. But mostly, I liked knowing he was here because I'd decided he should be. A permanent reminder of who held the strings.

My shoulders stiffened. The hair on the back of my neck prickled. I heard her the moment she entered the building. I left the bar for my office, telling myself I didn't want her to feel intimidated by her boss's watchful gaze. I'd remained glued to the clock, and now that she was here, I couldn't get out of the room fast enough.

"Everyone surviving, or do we need a necromancer for second shift?" she said to the others by way of greeting. I had to put on music to try to drown out her voice. I was glued to the time once more. Now that she'd arrived, I had to count every second until closing time before I could justify popping out to see her again.

She was funny. She was considerate. She was good at her job.

It was maddening.

I finally sauntered from my office with slow, purposeful steps at twenty-to-close.

Kit was still hard at work. She moved with a kind of energy I hadn't seen in a long time. She was so alive, so unaware of what existed just beneath the surface of this world. A part of me wanted to keep her that way—untouched, ignorant of the darkness. But another, stronger part, wanted to pull her into the shadows, to see if her light could survive it.

She turned, catching me staring, and I held her gaze, a slow, coy smile curving my lips. I saw the blush rise on her cheeks, her eyes widening slightly before she hurriedly looked away, nearly dropping the tray of drinks she was holding in her flustered rush. She was delightful.

Cain shifted beside me, drawing my attention back to the present. "Can I...get you anything?" he asked, his voice a grumble that betrayed his reluctance to speak.

I sighed. "No, Cain. Just try to look less constipated." I waved him off. He straightened slightly, his face going blank once more.

The minutes ticked by, each one slower than the last, and finally, the clock struck closing time. The last of the patrons filtered out, leaving only the staff to clean up and close down. I returned to my office, pretending to go over paperwork while I watched the security cameras, my eyes tracking Kit's every movement. She was the second-to-last to leave, taking her time as she gathered her things, chatting briefly with Jensen before he waved and disappeared out the back door.

I slipped out of my office, locking the door behind me. Kit was at the front door, fiddling with the lock, and I made my way over, my heels clicking softly against the floor.

"Need a hand?" I asked, my voice low, and she jumped slightly, turning to face me.

"Oh, hey," she said. "No, I've got it. Just...being finicky tonight."

I could tell I made her nervous, but wasn't sure if it was the good kind or the bad. I brushed against the bare skin of her wrist, briefly feeling her pulse before I gently took the keys from her hand. She nearly dropped them at my touch, which pleased me more than I could explain.

I stepped closer. I was making too much eye contact, but to hell with it. Her breath quickened as she took shallow sips of air, my perfume undoubtedly on her tongue.

"I wanted to thank you, you know," I said, doing my best to sound casual. "For the other night. Checking in on me. It's not often someone does that."

"With..." Her gaze shot to my henchman. "With *that* guy? I have to say I was...surprised to see him."

"Don't worry," I replied, "He's here to pay penance." Then to him, I said, "You'll never be disrespectful to a woman for as long as you live, will you, Cain?"

"No ma'am," he said, heels clicking together, spine straightening, as if I was the drill sergeant in his private military.

"Do you have anything to say to Kit?"

I hated how unnaturally he turned his neck. He belonged in a goddamn horror movie with his stilted *Exorcist*-like head movements. Still, he coughed up his line flawlessly.

"I was so inappropriate," he said to Kit. "You shouldn't forgive me. My behavior was disgusting. But I'm making good of the family's security business by spending some time in the trenches. I could use the humbling."

She was almost too stunned to speak. Almost.

"Good," she said at last.

"Again," I said, waving him away, "thank you, Kit."

She blinked, her cheeks flushing. "Oh, for the other night? It was nothing, really. I just...wanted to make sure you were okay. Women have to look out for each other, right? Especially with..."

Her sentence drifted. She did that a lot. I wonder if she was thoughtful, or shy, or just distracted by her internal world.

I smiled, leaning in just slightly. "Well, I appreciate it," I said, letting my gaze drop to her lips, then back to her eyes. "I agree, more than you know. I have your back."

She swallowed, her eyes widening just a fraction, and I could hear the way her pulse quickened, the slight hitch in her breath. "Th-thanks," she stammered.

I watched her for another moment, then stepped back, giving her space. "Goodnight, Kit," I said, my voice soft.

"Goodnight, Ms. Volkova," she replied, her voice barely a whisper.

Ouch.

I recovered as smoothly as I could. "Just Narya. For you, anyway."

I turned, making my way back to my office, a smile playing on my lips. As soon as I was out of sight, I headed for the side door, where Cain met me at the car.

"She's leaving now," I said, slipping into the back seat. "Keep a three-car distance. I don't want her to know we're following."

Cain grunted in acknowledgment, pulling away from the curb as Kit's car came into view. We trailed her through the darkened streets, the neon lights of the city casting long shadows across the pavement. She drove with a kind of casual confidence. I imagined her fingers drumming on the steering wheel in time with some unfamiliar femme alt-rock.

There was something about her, something that made it

impossible to look away. She was so...human. So alive. And I wanted to know everything about her.

After a while, she pulled into a run-down apartment complex, the kind of place that hadn't seen a fresh coat of paint in decades. I frowned, watching as she parked and got out, her eyes darting around as if checking to see if anyone was watching. Her silhouette passed under the amber pool of streetlight as she fished for her keys. She didn't see us, parked across the street, the car hidden in the shadows.

"She lives here?" Cain muttered, his brow furrowing.

"Seems so," I said, my voice thoughtful. I watched as she disappeared inside, the door closing behind her. I waited, my senses on high alert, listening for any sign of movement. I clocked a man stumbling from the pressing shadows toward her building.

Moments later, a buzz, the sound of someone pressing the intercom, cut through the quiet. A man's voice, slurred slightly, asking for "Lola." My eyes narrowed, my attention sharpening. Kit's voice came next, muffled but clear enough for me to hear. She was using a pseudonym.

The door unlocked, and the man went inside. I watched, my jaw clenching slightly as I pieced it together.

"Fuck."

Cain turned around. "What's wrong, boss?"

I seethed. "She's escorting."

"And that's… a problem?"

I looked out the window. I couldn't explain to this zombified shell of a loser that yes, it was a *huge* problem. I couldn't have her out here risking herself without protection. She was clearly taking in-calls from her apartment, which meant no one would hear her scream if there was trouble, and no one would know until the next day if her heart stopped beating. At the same time, this protective, maternal relationship wasn't one I wanted with her.

I had never had feelings for someone who wandered into my bar and handed me a resume. I hadn't intended to think twice about her when I'd hired her. Sure, she was beautiful, but then again, I was an art collector.

I can't quite explain what had happened, or when things had changed. But I was already her boss at the speakeasy. I was steeped in selfishness with how vehemently I didn't want to swoop in and save her from her unsafe practices, if only because I couldn't stand the idea of a second power imbalance. Dating the owner of the bar was rough. Dating your Madame? That was morally corrupt on every level.

Maybe it was fair. After all, why would I deserve happiness?

An hour later, the man left, his steps unsteady as he made his way back to his car. I watched him drive off, my attention returning to the building. Thirty minutes passed, and then Kit emerged, her head down, her shoulders hunched as she made her way to her car.

"She's on the move again," I said, my voice tight. "Follow her."

Cain nodded, pulling away from the curb, keeping a careful distance as we trailed her through the city. This time, she led us to a different neighborhood, one that was cleaner, quieter. She parked in front of a condominium complex comprised of glass and concrete and steel.

My gaze darted to the dimly lit shape moving in the window to the right of the closed door—a man I recognized from her socials. The fucker's name was Andy, and he was her boyfriend. He said something to her, his voice too soft for me to hear, and she nodded, stepping inside. The door closed behind them, and I felt a strange, bitter taste in my mouth.

"Drive," I said, my voice sharp. Cain glanced at me, his brow furrowing, but he didn't argue, pulling away from the condo and heading back towards the club.

I leaned back in my seat, my eyes closing as I replayed the

night in my mind. Kit was escorting. She was in a relationship. She was so goddamn mortal. The young woman had her whole life ahead of her. She was so breakable and yet so willing to put herself in danger, to live on the edge of something she may not fully understand.

And for the death of me, I can't get her out of my head.

Dearest Cetina—

I'm scared for her. Kit, I mean. Some traumatic wounds don't heal, no matter how much time passes. But there are enough Jack the Rippers targeting sex workers to fill a Lollapalooza—that joke would be funnier to you if you were both alive in this century and also knew her working name. I know I'm not just drawn to her out of that same urge to protect I felt the day I lost you. After all, I liked her before I knew. But fuck, if this hasn't complicated things. I don't want to look into her face and see yours.

You deserved so much better.

They all deserved better.

With all my love, forever,
Yours

CHAPTER 4

THESE MEN COULD USE SOME CULLEN'

KIT

The sun was already high when I stumbled out of Andy's bedroom, his old band t-shirt hanging off one shoulder. He was in the kitchen, flipping pancakes in his usual distracted way, his phone propped up against the toaster, streaming gameplay on YouTube. He grinned when he saw me, and the space lit with carefree joy. I paused in the doorway, feeling a strange tug at my chest.

We weren't fighting. That was nice, right? He was in a good mood, humming some late 90s rock song, and I was grateful we could just...be, without the tension that seemed to bubble up between us more and more lately. And yet, even with him happy, I was still walking on eggshells to keep the peace. We were never truly happy. Not in the way we used to be. There was an emptiness that hung between us, like we were just going through the motions because it was easier than admitting how broken we were. Then again, perhaps he didn't know we were fractured. It was hard to picture someone like him being self-reflective enough to understand that nothing about us was healthy.

"Mornin', babe," Andy said. "Hungry? I made pancakes."

Barefoot and pantsless, I slipped past him to the coffee pot. I caught a glimpse of the purple batter while filling a cup. "Blueberry pancakes?"

"I know what you like," he winked.

His attention shifted back to his phone, and I watched him for a moment, my stomach twisting. I hated that I was so cynical now, so ready to read into every gesture, every smile. I loved blueberry pancakes. I also loved when he woke up before me to make breakfast. In moments like these, I thought maybe I'd been exaggerating my impressions of Andy as a bad guy. He was...fine. When he wasn't angry, I remembered why I'd fallen for him in the first place.

My phone buzzed on the table.

"Who's texting you first thing on a Sunday?" Andy asked.

I snatched it before Andy could see the notification was from a burner app.

New message from: Markus79.

I opened it, quickly skimming the text. It was a prospective client, asking about availability for later that evening.

"It's one of the girls from the bar," I lied, silencing the phone and flipping it face down. "She was just texting to remind me that we're supposed to get a drink at seven. I don't think I'll be home for dinner tonight, babe. I'm sorry."

My body flooded with adrenaline as I waited for the screaming to start. He knew why I wouldn't be home.

Andy's brows furrowed. The batter sizzled, then went quiet as the cooked pancake began to smoke and burn. Every second of silence took an eternity. I held my breath as I waited for him to say something.

"What? Since when? You made plans without asking me?"

Familiar tension twisted within me, but I still experienced a modicum of relief that he wasn't outright yelling. I knew I conflated these moments of reprieve with the sort of joy I used to feel when he was nice to me. If he was still the person he'd led me to believe when we started dating, I wouldn't have to curate my words to avoid triggering him. I could have told him who I was meeting, shared my location for safety, and joked about my nights in the industry. But he hadn't been that man for a long time. Now, it was all I could do to stop him from yelling. I forced myself to keep my tone light. "It was last minute. You and I haven't had the chance to chat."

He stared at me for a moment, then shrugged, turning back to the stove. "Whatever. I guess that means more time for me to finish this campaign." He gave me a quick smile, and I could see the relief in his eyes. He didn't actually want me there—not in his life, or in his apartment—not really.

I nodded, swallowing back the bitterness that rose in my throat. "Yeah. More time for you."

The air turned awkward and heavy. I expected Andy to set the dirty dishes in the sink and return to his game, but he seemed in good spirits today. A smile played on his lips. "I made you pancakes. Maybe you could give me a little snack in return?" He stepped closer, his hands brushing against my hips, and I knew what he wanted. I closed my eyes, letting him pull me in.

I wasn't proud of myself for this, but as his fingers dug into my hips, I was reminded of why I'd stayed in this relationship so long past its expiration. I loved sex, and he was fantastic in the sack.

He flipped me around so my tummy pressed into the counter's hard edge. I planted my palms on the cool marble. He traced claiming kisses along my spine, mouth going down while his hand traveled up my back. He knotted his fingers in my hair, and I gasped at the sharp tug. He straightened, kissing my neck, my cheek, nibbling on my ear before using his rough grasp on my hair to force my lips onto his. A familiar throb began to pound between my legs. I closed my eyes as he shoved the t-shirt up as far as he could and yanked down my panties.

They caught on the curve of my thigh, but it was just enough for him to enter.

His cock was enormous, and I was dick whipped. I loved everything about it. I loved the way it looked, the way it felt, the way it hit my G-spot like no one ever had. I loved the oxytocin and dopamine it provided now that there was no other source of joy in this loveless relationship. I bit my lip hard as he shoved himself in, groaning if only to keep from screaming.

"You like that?" he asked, slapping my ass with a sharp smack.

"Fuck yes," I moaned, and I meant it.

He began to pound into me. I lowered my cheek to the cool marble, wishing I was resting my face against pale, pillowing breasts. I cried out as he came within a fraction of an inch of bottoming out, but he always knew just where to stop, just how hard to go, just how to plow into me to bring me to orgasm.

"Whose pussy is this?" He growled.

But I only saw a slick, blonde ponytail, ice-chipped eyes, painted lips, and a scandalously low-cut silk top.

"I said," he yanked my hair back, "whose pussy is this?"

Eyes still closed, I looked directly into my boss's face as I whispered. "Yours. It's yours."

My apartment was a shithole, but I liked to pretend it was artsy and eclectic. The truth was, no one lived here by choice, and I wasn't exactly pulling in high-end Johns with this rundown in-call cesspool. I wasn't dumb enough to hang anything personal or identifying on the walls, but the remaining art felt more like a college dorm than a woman in her mid-twenties. I tidied, re-applied deodorant, fixed my mascara, and was still brushing my teeth when the buzzer went off.

"This is Lola," I said.

"Hey, Lola. John, here."

"Come on up." I spit the toothpaste and waited by the door.

My nerves were already on edge when he came swaggering in like he owned the place, his cologne so strong it made my eyes water.

"Nice place," he said, his gaze raking over me, a smirk playing on his lips. "Not what I expected, but nice."

Liar.

I gave him a tight smile, trying to push down the unease that was building in my chest. "Go ahead and take a quick shower while I snatch us a couple of drinks. What do you want? Beer, or a seltzer maybe?"

"Got any whiskey?" He took a seat on the bed.

My lower lip puckered in feigned sympathy. "It's not good practice to take open drinks from clients or providers, so to be respectful of safety, let's stick to cans. Okay?"

"No whiskey *and* you're making me shower? You saying you think I'm gonna drug you and I stink?"

Yes. "Of course not. It's standard practice for both clients and providers to shower before a date."

He grabbed my hand and yanked me to him. I stumbled into the space beside him. Alarm bells rang in my head, but I had a few tricks to deescalate before I went nuclear.

"You're not my first hooker," he said. "I know what is and isn't common practice. And if we get in the shower, we're going together, and I'll absolutely be fucking you in the ass."

I tried to remain calm, but he wasn't making it easy. His hands were all over me, and I felt that familiar panic bubbling up—the same feeling I'd had the first time I realized Andy wasn't who I thought he was. The realization that I was in too deep, that I'd made a mistake. If I didn't follow my instincts with this guy, things could turn out far worse than losing a couple hundred bucks.

"Hey," I said, my voice sharper than I intended. "Let's take a step back."

The man looked at me, his eyes narrowing. "What? Why?"

"I'm not feeling comfortable, and I don't think we're a good match," I said, trying to keep my tone steady. "I can recommend providers better suited to your needs, but I think you should go."

He scoffed, his face darkening. "Are you serious? I paid for this."

"The deposit donation is non-refundable, but I won't charge you for the hour. You paid for my time," I said, standing up, trying to keep my distance. "And I'm ending it now. Get out."

His expression twisted, and for a moment, I thought he might actually lunge at me. Instead, he started shouting, obscenities spilling from his lips as he grabbed the lamp from the side table and hurled it across the room.

I flinched, my hands trembling as I reached for the taser I kept in the bedside drawer. "Get out!" I shouted, my voice shaking. "Get the hell out of my apartment before I call the cops."

"Call the cops and say what? Call the cops and get thrown in prison for prostitution?"

"Try it," I said, venom on my tongue. "Try me and see which one of us they haul away."

For a moment, he stared at me, his eyes wide with rage, but then he turned, muttering curses under his breath as he stormed out, slamming the door behind him. I sank onto the bed, my heart pounding, my hands still shaking as I tried to steady my breathing.

"Shit," I whispered, my eyes stinging. I needed a drink—something to take the edge off, to drown out the mess that had just unfolded. I stumbled to the kitchen, yanking open the cupboards, but they were empty. No gin, no vodka, no tequila.

Just canned seltzers and beers, and my safe-for-client drinks weren't strong enough to cut it.

"Great. Just fucking great." I slammed the cupboard door shut, running a hand through my hair. I needed to get out, to clear my head. Maybe grab a drink somewhere that didn't feel like it was closing in on me.

I grabbed my keys, slipping my jacket on as I headed for the door. Seattle was out of its false-spring, and the January freeze had returned with a vengeance. Winter air hit me as I stepped outside, and I took a deep breath, letting it calm me. It was quiet, the street empty except for a few parked cars, their head-lights off. I made my way toward my car, my thoughts a jumble of anger, fear, and frustration. If it got any colder, this drizzle would turn into an arctic sleet, coating the hilly city with impossible ice.

I was halfway across the street when headlights flashed. A roaring engine sliced my false sense of security in half. My heart leaped into my throat, and I froze, my feet glued to the asphalt as the car hurtled toward me.

John.

It was like everything slowed down. The headlights were so bright, and I could feel my body lock up, my muscles refusing to move. I was going to die. The thought hit me like a punch to the gut, and I couldn't do anything but watch as the car got closer, the driver's face a blur behind the windshield.

This was it.

My life didn't flash before my eyes.

It was something else that sprinted into view. A confusing blur of blue, black, and silver. The grim reaper's blur was that of long hair, of a cinched waist, of impossibly high heels. I'd expected childhood memories, but I only heard a loud, femi-nine growl as the confusing silhouette cried out in the second it took to dash between me and the oncoming vehicle.

The driver slammed on his brakes, car fish-tailing at the last second, but it wasn't enough to avoid me and the tall, feminine blur. The crack of metallic impact was so loud, I thought the vehicle exploded. My knees crumpled beneath me as I fell. I felt something grab me—a hand on the back of my head, cradling me just before my skull cracked against the pavement.

I looked up, my vision dimming, and saw her. Narya. Her face calm and her eyes cold as she turned away from me, her stilettos clicking softly against the asphalt. She moved toward the driver, the man was sprawled on the ground, blood dripping from a gash on his forehead. My heart pounded, and I tried to focus, tried to stay conscious, but everything was slipping away, the world fading to black.

The last thing I heard was the man's voice, choked and desperate, begging for his life.

Chapter 5

Boss Bitch of the Damned

Narya

Seattle's rain turned to ice on the windshield. The car ahead of us tried to brake at the intersection but skidded through four lanes of traffic without stopping.

My blood boiled. Or, whoever's blood was in me, boiled. "Are you trying to take the bridge? Cain, you fucking *idiot*, we're in an ice storm! Do *not* get us over water!"

"She needs an ER, and the Capitol Hill campus is on that steep incline, boss, and I—"

I punctured his headrest with my nails. Kit was unconscious in my lap. "We're ten minutes from the Center. Get us there."

"The where?"

He was lucky I enjoyed the luxury of a private driver enough to tolerate his broad-spectrum uselessness. I punched an address into my phone and watched as it appeared on the console. "The vampire center, you imbecile."

"But Kit and I are human," his eyes. "We can't go to a vampire center."

"Don't you *dare* try to tell me how to handle my kind." I'd been looking for a reason to rip his head off from the moment I'd met him, whether or not he was a mindless henchman. This was far too much backtalk from someone I'd virtually lobotomized.

He said nothing as he exited the interstate and steered us downtown. Headlights reflected off the black ice that coated the streets. Cars bumped into one another like they were children's toys. Cain turned onto Pike just as a tow truck flipped onto its side and slammed into us.

The horrid scraping, cracking, and popping was like something out of a war zone.

I reacted on instinct, curling around Kit, leaving Cain to defend himself as our vehicle crumpled. It crashed down on me, molding around me as I proved more resilient than the titanium, fiberglass, and steel. In that moment, I was a snow leopard, feral, icy, and lethal. I sprung from the twisted wreckage, breaking through the shattered cage that had once been a mint-condition Maserati. I was barely aware of Kit's doll-like form as I threw her over my shoulder and carried her from the disaster.

"Holy shit, lady, your arm!" The dazed tow truck driver slipped on the ice as he stumbled toward us. I could smell the vodka in his pores from here. "Are you okay?"

"Ah, fuck." My left arm lay detached on the ground. Perfectly manicured fingers twitched as I tried to flex my phantom limb. I set Kit down, grabbed my arm, and was on top of the driver before he knew what was happening. "Driving drunk in an ice storm? You almost killed us!"

"I'm sorry! I..." the rest of his words garbled as I ripped his throat out with my teeth. I held my arm to the socket as I drank deeply, satisfied as the fibers stitched together. I came up with a satisfied smack as I drained the last drop, then used his jean jacket to wipe the blood from my face.

Cain was still army crawling from the wreck like a pathetic insect. I rolled my eyes and threw him over my shoulder like a potato sack, then picked Kit up as carefully as I could. We'd be safer on foot, anyway. Seattle called every drizzle a Snowpocalypse. They'd have never lived through the treacherous twenty-foot blizzards in Transylvania's Carpathian Mountains before snowplows, emergency survival kits, and widespread electricity.

My face was still smeared with blood. I was moving at inhumane speeds. Fuck it, if humans saw me, they'd have to chalk it up to wintery delusions. Moments later, I was at the Center. The brutalist architecture of the thirty-story building hid it in plain sight, claiming its windowlessness was necessary for protecting the telephone lines and switches. Should anything happen to the building, there'd be a communications blackout throughout the city. This was true of half of the fortress's floors, but more importantly, the solid concrete allowed the city's vampires a place to duck away from prying eyes.

Thumbprint.

Retinal scan.

Security code.

Hulking undead meathead escorting me into the decontamination room.

Hulking undead meathead asking too many questions about the zombie and the unconscious human who may or may not be the single most important thing in my world.

Hulking undead meathead pinned to the wall, cowing for mercy at a vampire three hundred years his elder and six times his strength, narrowly escaping execution thanks to the hasty opening of the security doors.

"Narya! Violent as ever, I see," preened a familiar voice.

"Aaliyah," I said without looking at her. My eyes were still on the meathead.

"Let him go," Aaliayah chastised. "He made a mistake. He's a man, after all."

I narrowed my eyes to let him know that the next time he irritated me would be his last, then let him slump to the floor.

A glittering, golden bra, elaborate headdress, and sheer, floor-length skirt adorned the woman leaning casually in the doorway. She was dressed for ceremony. I wasn't sure what I'd interrupted, but I immediately regretted my decision.

"I'd ask if you brought us a snack to celebrate the Cold Moon, but I assume that's why poor Viktor nearly lost his head."

"He barely had a head to start with," I muttered. "I'm looking for Arthur. Is he here?"

"He is." She looked at me suspiciously. Arthur enjoyed playing with human anatomy the same way humans enjoyed playing with tarot, crystal balls, and Ouija boards. He was better at it than any of us and could sense a malady from simply a sniff, a touch, a listen.

"Take me to him,"

She folded her arms across her chest. "Oh, come on. After all that's passed between us? No, *'I miss you, Aaliyah', 'I want you back in my bed, Aaliyah', 'I can't stop thinking about that thing you do with your tongue, Aaliyah'.*"

"She needs help," I said, scooping Kit back into my arms. "Concussion, broken bones, I'm not sure. She's been unconscious for too long."

"Help her yourself."

I hedged. "I don't want her…connected to me in that way. Not unless she wants it. It can be a lot for a human."

Lore and pop culture were locked in an arms race to convince humans that vampires had fantastic powers, healing blood, and life-saving abilities. Our blood was closer to a virus than some magic potion. The virus, however, overrode imperfections in human DNA which often lead to positive side effects, like mending the broken, stamping out disease, or bringing someone back from the brink of death. Without committing to the transition, however, a human became a shell of themselves, precisely like Cain. It was challenging to achieve a perfect outcome when crafting a mindless servant, so few of us tried.

I, however, was not a quitter.

"Then change her." Aaliyah shrugged away from the doorframe.

"She doesn't even know what I am," I said quietly. "Are you going to help me or not?"

Aaliyah chewed on her lip. "Not. But tonight's a reaping. Every vampire in the city is here. I'm sure someone will help you." She paused over Cain's body as he looked on with a stupefied expression. "And, what's this? He doesn't smell alive, nor is he one of us."

I wondered if I looked as annoyed as I felt. "He's dead. The only thing keeping him ticking is his connection to me."

"Without transformation?"

"Without transformation."

"How curious," she said. "The others may be satisfied enough with your little monster to overlook your...*human*."

I held Kit in my arms while dragging Cain on the ground behind me like a discarded toy. I hadn't been to the Center in twelve years. Aaliyah had wanted to rise to power together, and though I'd enjoyed our time in bed and her vision for the future, I had not developed the same attachment she had. Things had not ended well, to say the least.

The building was precisely as I remembered it.

Unremarkable rows of cables and servers and coolants as far as the eye could see. A nondescript service elevator. A deeply normal-looking panel that would take us as high or as low as the building appeared to go. A simultaneous press of button 1 and button 3 sent us to the otherwise numberless 13th floor. A tasteful lobby, too upscale for a windowless tech building, but still not quite suspicious. And finally, a second set of retinal and thumb scans and passcodes to enter The Hall.

I hadn't attended a full moon ceremony in ages, and if I hadn't been panicking in the midst of an ice storm, I certainly wouldn't have brought Kit and Cain here tonight. The throng was thirty vampires strong, all in various states of undress. Humans accompanied them on all sides. Some looked like willing, enthusiastic participants. Others appeared chained at the ankle, whimpering for their lives.

It was such a gauche cliché.

"Where's Arthur?" I asked, planting my feet by the door. I wasn't going to take Kit a single step deeper into this den of beasts.

The atmosphere in The Hall was suffocating. I scanned the crowd, every sense within me on high alert.

I didn't clock Arthur until he appeared at my side. His thin, hunched shoulders struck a Rasputin-like shape above my humans, his expression set in that familiar mask of curiosity and disapproval.

"Narya." He said, wringing his papery hands like a comic book villain. If I hadn't known him for years and sought him out on purpose, I would have deemed him the very picture of sinister. "So, you're back after all this time, and you brought us a girl."

I'd known bringing Kit here would be dangerous, but I hadn't had a choice. Not really.

"Tell me where to carry her."

"You can't come." Arthur stepped closer, lowering his voice. "Another vampire's presence will sully the results."

This didn't ring true, but I didn't know enough about this process to understand why. I stopped myself from arguing when I took another look at the room. She couldn't stay in the main hall.

I clenched my jaw, eyes narrowing at the sight of Kit, then back to Arthur. "I'm just supposed to hand her over to you?"

He regarded me slowly, as if truly seeing me at last. "Who is she to you?" When I didn't respond, he said, "This other human of yours may join us. He won't have the vampiric brainwaves that interfere with my practice."

"Fine," I said, my voice clipped. Then to Cain, I said, "Guard her with whatever's left of your pathetic life."

"Off we go, then." Arthur took Kit from my arms, beckoning Cain to follow. "Enjoy the ceremony, Ms. Volkova."

I stood still for a moment, watching the retreating figures until they disappeared through an arched doorway. My chest felt tight, a strange mix of anger and worry gnawing at me. While we'd been speaking, the atmosphere in The Hall had shifted. Music had begun to play, though I couldn't spy its source. There was a thickness to the air, something like perfume and sex and incense. As the anticipation reached a fever pitch, the candles burned brighter, their flames swaying in sync with the rhythmic pounding from the music that seemed to be getting louder and louder. I moved deeper into the crowd on primal instinct, the energy around me almost palpable—an electric buzz that seemed to seep into my skin, winding its way through my veins.

The debauchery roared from all sides, vampires feeding from the throng of humans scattered throughout the room. The scent of blood hung heavy in the air, mixing with the musk of power and desire. I surveyed the room, my senses dulled as if I'd already had too much to drink. I wondered if I could possibly be this blood drunk from the tow truck driver.

No, this buzz was the ceremony, the power of the Cold Moon, the ancient magic that bound us all. It felt like a drug, my mind foggy, my body moving without my conscious command.

The drums grew louder, the tempo increasing, and I felt myself pulled toward the center of The Hall. My feet moved of their own accord, my body swaying in time with the music, my eyes half-closed as I surrendered to the pull. I could feel the magic wrapping around me, seeping into my thoughts, my emotions—a heady mix of power and need.

I reached the center of the room, my gaze lifting, and there was Aaliyah. Had her eyes always been this bright? Her lips were so full. His body was…well, her body had always been amazing.

Had we been talking?

I had a feeling as though I'd lost a word on the tip of my tongue, misplaced a friend's name, or entered a room and forgotten why I was there. Aaliyah was a familiar life raft, something concrete in the current of bodies and music. She moved closer, her hands finding their way to my waist, body pressing into mine.

Her breath was hot against my neck. Her lips grazed my skin. A shiver ran through me, my body reacting to her touch. It was familiar. It was…good? I liked it when she touched me. I was sure that was true, though I couldn't remember why.

Her hands moved lower, her fingers teasing, and I let out a soft gasp, my mind a haze of instinct. I turned, my lips meeting hers, the kiss deepening as the magic of the Cold Moon wrapped around us, drum thumping, binding us in a moment that felt outside of time, outside of anything else.

My vision blurred. Memories from fifty years prior assaulted me. Aaliyah interrupting my first kill in the Pacific Northwest, welcoming me to Seattle, introducing me to the Center. Aaliyah with her dress pooling around her ankles, her hands between my thighs, her fangs tracing sharp lines from my knee to my sex. Aaliyah pulling my hair, me pushing her against the wall, her tearing my clothes to shreds, her scream-ing. Aaliyah swirling her tongue around my clit, then sucking gently as she nudged her fingers inside.

Twirl, suck, twirl, suck, twirl, suck.

Fifteen years of toxic fights, of dick measuring contests between the two of us, of hate fucking and slaughtering our way through the population, until I put it to an end.

I brushed against the cold metal of her bra, and she saved me the trouble, unhooking it and baring her breasts to the room. The bodies around us were in similar states of undress, everyone moving in tandem as if we were performing the steps to some ancient dance. I lowered my mouth to her collarbone, her sternum, her breast. My tongue moved against the light brown peak of her nipple, popping one into my mouth while my hand worked against her free breast. Her hands were on my belt in an instant, undoing my pants. I knew I'd be drenched before her palm grazed my sex through the silk of my panties.

I groaned against her. "Fuck…"

"See?" She said. "I knew you missed that thing I did with my tongue."

"Mmm," I tried to murmur in agreement, but I was enjoying the slow circles of her hand too much. Wait, what did she mean? Why did I miss it? Why would I ever let her stop? She was fantastic in bed. We were feral any time we were together. We'd trashed hotels across North America and most of Europe. We'd shredded hundreds of thousands of dollars of designer clothes beyond repair, all teeth, claws, and sex.

"I knew that human was nothing special. And once Arthur is done with her, well…you'll have nothing to worry about."

I snatched her hand, forcing it to stop its circles. "What the fuck did you just say?"

"Oh, playing the aggressor, now? I like when we switch."

I squeezed her wrist so hard I heard a bone pop. She gasped, eyes widening. "Narya, what are you doing?"

"Kit. Where's Kit?"

She laughed, fangs glistening as her cackle cut through the music. "You can't be serious."

I tightened my squeeze, shattering her forearm. This time her scream was punctuated with a hiss. "Tell me where she is. *Now.*"

CHAPTER 6

OVER MY DEAD BODY

KIT

My eyes fluttered open, my vision swimming as I tried to focus. The ceiling above me was an unfamiliar shade of gray, and the air felt sterile, cold. I blinked, my gaze shifting to the side, and that's when I saw the Page Turner's new bouncer.

Cain was lying on a table like mine, his eyes wide open, staring blankly at the ceiling. For a second, I thought he was awake, that he was just...waiting. But something was wrong. He wasn't blinking. He wasn't moving. And then I noticed the figure bent over him, a slender silhouette working with deliberate precision.

A sickening, slurping sound preceded the wet thump of organs in a bowl. The thin figure marched to the far side of the room to examine the xrays mounted to a square, white light. On the right, a square, male torso. On the left...could that be mine? I looked at Cain's unseeing form once more. His intestines had been plucked from his belly like they was sausage.

My stomach lurched, bile rising in my throat, and I clapped my hand over my mouth to keep from screaming. The thin man began to turn and I squeezed my eyes shut. I needed a plan before he knew I was awake. I had to get out of here.

"No good, dear," a voice said, calm and smooth, cutting through the fog of panic. "I knew you were awake the moment your breathing changed."

I turned my head, my heart pounding, and looked at the man standing beside Cain. He was looking at me now, his eyes sharp, a cold smile curving his lips. He wiped his hands on a cloth, his gaze never leaving mine.

I scrambled to sit up, my body protesting the movement, but something stopped me—handcuffs, cold and unyielding, clamped around my wrists, holding me to the table. I pulled against them, my breath coming in ragged gasps, panic clawing at my chest.

"Where am I?" I demanded, voice trembling. "What are you going to do to me?"

The man stepped closer, his eyes glinting in the dim light. "My name is Arthur," he said, his tone polite, almost conversational. "And as for what I'm going to do to you...well." He flashed his teeth, and my heart stuttered as I saw two dagger-sharp fangs. "I'm going to drink your blood, of course. But first —" He paused, tilting his head, his smile widening. "It's the full moon. Let's celebrate by playing a little doctor, shall we?"

Terror surged through me, and I pulled harder against the handcuffs, my eyes wide. "No—no, please—"

But before I could finish, the door to the room burst open. My head snapped toward the noise, and my breath caught in my throat.

A scarlet statue of dripping blood stood in the doorway, her eyes blazing. Narya was soaked from head to toe, dark liquid staining her clothes, her skin, her hair. The surgeon, the blood, the lifeless gaze, the threatening, beautiful woman soaked in the terrible, vermillion liquid... this had to be a nightmare.

Arthur's mouth opened, but he didn't get a chance to say

anything. Narya closed the distance a blur of movement. Her hand whipped out, fingers closing around his throat. With a horrifying rip, she tore his esophagus from his throat. He remained on his feet for a full second before collapsing to the ground, now as lifeless as the bouncer. Narya towered over him, disembodied esophagus dangling like a trophy, fangs protruding as she hissed at his corpse.

I stared, my heart pounding, my mind struggling to keep up with what had just happened. She bent over the man only as long as it took for her to pluck a silver key from his pocket.

Narya turned to me, her expression softening, and I opened my mouth, trying to find words, trying to make sense of any of this. "We...we have to go," I stammered, voice barely audible. "We have to get out of here—"

"No need to run," she said, her voice calm, almost gentle. She moved closer, her eyes meeting mine. "The others are dead. We can take as long as we like."

I blinked, confusion and fear warring in my chest. "Why...why are you doing this?"

Narya hesitated. "Because...you remind me of someone. Someone I lost. Someone I never thought I'd get over. And if you never want to see me again after tonight, that's fine. But I couldn't let you die. Not now that I'm strong enough to do something about it."

My chest tightened, a strange mix of emotions swirling inside me—fear, confusion, gratitude. I didn't know what to say, didn't know how to process any of this.

Narya moved closer, her hands gentle as she unlocked the handcuffs, freeing me from the table. I sat up, my body trembling. She helped me to my feet, her arm around my waist, steadying me.

"Let's go," she said.

And because I had no possible backup plan, I had no choice: I followed.

"Oh, um," she extended a wet arm to stop me. "You might want to close your eyes for this next room. Some things you can't unsee."

"It's hard to imagine it getting any worse," I said.

"Then maybe you don't have a very vivid imagination."

I complied, nearly gagging at the wet, squishing sounds beneath my feet as she led me across what felt like a very large room. My hand flew to plug my nose as I was hit with a wave of decay.

"Oh, the smell," came her voice, presumably reacting to my attempts not to choke on the scent. "Death keeled over takes on a new meaning when it takes some of these fuckers ten, fifty, one hundred years to die. Here we go, big step." I refused to look as she helped me over a motionless bump of fabric and goo that felt an awful lot like a leg.

I opened my eyes once I heard the ding of an elevator, but it was a moment too soon. A pile of ruby-red carnage seared itself into my memory the moment before the doors shut, and soft jazz began to play.

I didn't speak as we made our way out of the building, the cold night air hitting me like a slap to the face. I shivered, my body still weak, my mind a haze of confusion and fear. Narya led me to the curb, her eyes scanning the empty street.

"Where are we going?" I asked.

"I'm calling an Uber."

I gaped. "Looking like *that?*"

"My Maserati is scrap metal," she said, her voice dry. "And you're too mortal to make it all the way back to mine in the cold."

We stood in silence as the bitingly cold wind whipped through the streets, the only sound the distant hum of traffic. The rain had warmed, if only by a few degrees, and the sheets of ice that had covered the streets were already beginning to melt, the water running in rivulets down the pavement.

The Uber arrived a few minutes later, and we climbed in, the driver giving us a wide-eyed look but saying nothing. I caught a glimpse of myself in the rearview mirror—my clothes were rumpled, my face pale, my eyes wide with shock. I looked like someone who'd just escaped a horror movie, and maybe I had. Except I'd brought the villain with me.

The driver remained silent as the car moved through the city. The soft murmur of the Cab News playing on an iPad draped over the back of his seat. I stared at the screen, my heart skipping a beat when a familiar face flashed across it—a missing person's report for a man named Colby LeBlanc. A picture of Cain.

"Oops," Narya said, her voice tired.

I said nothing, though added this to my list of things to process once the world began to make sense again.

We pulled up in front of flashy high rise, the lights of the city reflecting off its glass facade. Narya leaned over the front seat, making overly intense eye contact with the driver, her voice low as she spoke.

"There's blood in your back seat," she said, her tone matter-of-fact. "An inconsiderate passenger was traveling from the butcher shop. Here's how you get your insurance to replace it for free." She gave him a few quick instructions, then turned to me, extending a bloody hand to help me out of the car.

I took her hand, my fingers trembling as I let her lead me out of the car.

I shot a nervous glance to the doorman.

"Don't worry about him," Narya said as we approached.

"Is he also…brainwashed?"

"Charmed, and no. But I tip him well enough not care. Hello, Daren." She flashed him a smile.

"Ms. Volkova," he said. He held the door for us, then rushed to the elevator. "Have a nice night."

I stared at her.

"I tip in hundreds," she said.

We rode the elevator without speaking, listening to the soft hum of the machinery. My mind was spinning, a thousand questions fighting for space, but none of them seemed to matter right now. Not after everything that had happened.

The elevator doors opened to reveal an elite, luxury penthouse, the space vast and beautifully decorated. A stark contrast to the chaos of the past few hours. I stepped out, my eyes taking in the plush furniture and the floor-to-ceiling windows that looked out over the city.

"So, you're a vampire, huh?" I said, my voice breaking the silence.

Narya sucked in a breath, her eyes meeting mine. "What gave it away?"

I let out a shaky laugh, my body trembling with exhaustion. "Are you going to eat me?"

"Well, not in the blood and gore sort of way..." Narya said, her lips quirking up into a tired smile. "Sorry. I'm sure you're not in the mood for jokes." She turned away, grabbing a towel from a nearby chair. "Let me wash off, then I'll get you home. Or, to your boyfriend's house. Or a hotel. Wherever you want to go."

I fidgeted. "Can I ask a few questions?"

The corner of Narya's lips tugged upward. "We don't sleep in coffins, we can't turn into bats, but we do, in fact, have to be invited into homes."

The information rolled around on my tongue like a chewy bit of meat. "Why?"

A single shoulder lifted. "I don't know if you believe in good or evil, but there seem to be some laws that govern the universe. One of them is: you have to choose the darkness, the darkness can't choose you."

"Except depression," I laughed.

"And when your boss stalks you," she agreed. "It's not a perfect metaphor."

I wasn't ready for the conversation to be over. "Why blood?"

"You mean, other than…because I'm a vampire?"

She was joking. I liked that. I nodded.

"We don't produce our own. The human body makes about two million new blood cells every second. The moment we die, so does our cell regeneration. So, we have to cheat." She tapped her too-sharp teeth. "Nature gave us a present. Like all apex carnivores, we get fangs to help us survive."

"And…" I hedged. "Last question. How were you able to… well, that other vampire…Was he not as strong as you? Whose blood are you currently covered in? What the fuck happened while I was—"

"That's one question? The American education system is in worse shape than I thought."

It would have been mean if her eyes hadn't softened. She knew I was upset. "I'm the oldest in the city. And now, perhaps, the only in the city. Now, if you don't mind," she gestured grandly to the disaster that was her ruined outfit.

"Oh my god, of course, of course." I ran my hands through my hair, anxious that I'd done something terribly rude. I didn't know the rules. Honestly, I was still a little too shell-shocked to care.

She moved toward the bathroom, bright red footprints soft against the polished floor. I stood there for a long moment, my eyes fixed on the door she'd left cracked open.

I pinched myself if only to prove I was awake.

I recited the alphabet, recited the month, the President, and pi to six places. I didn't seem to have a concussion, nor was there convincing evidence that I'd lost my mind.

I listened to the sound of running water.

She'd saved me. I wasn't sure how, or why, but the last thing I recalled was a psychotic client trying to run me down with his car. She'd put her body between me and the vehicle, and then when I'd woken up in a scene from *Saw*. She'd torn through scores of bodies to save me.

But why? I'd had bosses enjoy my presence in the workplace before, but this…well. This was supernatural.

I didn't even realize I'd started walking at first. I was moving on instinct, following an invisible pull from my place frozen in the living room to the slowly curling cloud of steam. I pushed the door open just a little more.

Narya was standing under the spray fully clothed, the water running red as it fought a losing battle against the blood-stained fabric. Her head was tilted back, her eyes closed. I stepped inside, the steam filling the room, the warmth wrapping around me, and without a word, I stepped into the shower.

Her eyes snapped open, her gaze meeting mine, surprise flickering across her face. I picked up the towel she had left draped over the edge of the shower, my hands trembling as I slowly began to wipe the blood away from her face. The steam made it hard to see, the water pouring down over both of us, but I focused on the task, on the feel of the fabric in my hand, the shape of her body beneath my touch.

Narya watched me, her expression shifting from surprise to something softer, something almost vulnerable. She let out a shaky breath, barely audible over the sound of the running water.

"And if I want to stay here tonight?" I asked, my voice catching in my throat.

Her breath hitched, her eyes widening slightly. She was silent for a long moment, her gaze locked on mine, and then she nodded, her voice soft, almost reverent. "Then…you'll stay here."

Dear Notes App—

Confused. Exhausted. Wet, and not in the fun way.
Scared, not in a way that makes sense.
Excited, but only in a way that I shouldn't be.
Hopeful, despite my better judgment, for the first time in a long time.

Kit

CHAPTER 7

THE FINAL NAIL IN THE COFFIN

NARYA

I didn't expect to sleep.

A human was in my room, and dawn had already crested. While overcast winters in Seattle protected me from the harshest rays of sun, I'd still made painstaking efforts to make sure that my house was a veritable air-tight, light-free coffin during the day.

Despite her initial romantic gesture of helping me rinse off, I didn't think a murdering spree would be an aphrodisiac for Kit. That, and once the adrenaline had worn off, she could barely keep her eyes open. I helped her to the bed, then spent two hours cleaning blood from every strand of hair, every curve, every crevice. By the time I tip-toed to the room, she was sound asleep and snoring ever so softly.

She'd stayed.

My fingers flew to my mouth, covering the near-giddy smile tugging at the corners of my lips. She hadn't only learned what I was, she'd also learned I could brainwash people—including her kidnapped, now-deceased coworker—and that I'd committed the sort of mass murder that usually made history books. She'd quite literally helped me wash the blood from my hands. And then she'd stayed.

I'd fought a lot of battles that night, but the willpower it took not to drape my arm around her in her sleep was Herculean.

I'd figure out the rest by sunset, but for now…this was no longer a crush, or an unhealthy obsession, or the sort of thing I'd have to pay a vampiric therapist to dissect for the next thousand years to come. This was real. And whatever it was, at least in part, she must have felt something, too.

I closed my eyes but knew sleep would not be finding me that day. So instead, I repeated the same two words over and over like a prayer: *she stayed, she stayed, she stayed.*

———————————

My eyes opened at 4:45 pm. I couldn't believe I'd fallen asleep beside her. It wasn't enough sleep, but winters in the Pacific Northwest were particularly long and dark. My body was instinctively attuned to the sunset after centuries of syncing my afterlife to dusk and dawn.

Sunlight was one thing that most lore and pop culture agreed upon. It fucking *hurt*, and the moment we were exposed, the clock for our survival started ticking. TV needed to make the death snappy, as they're only allotted an hour of air time, but whether or not we took ten seconds or ten minutes, we did, in fact, meet a fiery end.

A vampire from the Carpathians once told me that our kind was a metaphor for death, damnation, and darkness, which was why we craved lifeforce, were doomed to Hell, and were bested by the sun. The vampire had been a monk who'd been converted against his will, but explained his rationale for living as twofold: he now had eternity to do good deeds, and walking into the sun was considered suicide, which his faith didn't permit.

I felt like his god would make an exception.

Honestly, I didn't know why the sun killed us, as my kind wasn't exactly rife with scientists.

The darkened room came into focus, the silk sheets cool against my skin. I turned over, expecting to see her, and my heart sank when I realized Kit wasn't there.

For a moment, I just stared at the empty space beside me, my thoughts racing through possibilities. Had she left? Slipped away quietly without saying anything? Was she scared, or had she simply changed her mind about staying?

I snatched a remote from the bedside table and pressed the button to raise the apartment's blackout blinds, revealing the city beyond, a blur of windows, neon, and headlights. The Space Needle pierced the sky, its tip disappearing in cloud coverage. For a moment, I listened to the quiet noises of the city below. A muffled sound from the other room caught my attention.

I slipped out of bed, the floor cool beneath my feet, and moved silently toward the kitchen. Kit stood with her hands braced against the counter, a frying pan sitting uselessly on a cold stove, the coffee pot empty beside her. She looked lost, her brows drawn together in thought. It was the most beautiful face of confusion I'd ever seen.

"What are you doing?" I asked.

Kit looked up, undoubtedly startled by my cat-like silence. Her eyes met mine. She let out a small laugh, her expression almost embarrassed. "I wanted to make you breakfast," she said. "And then I remembered... Well, how does an overnight guest make blood? Do I...do you..." She trailed off, extending her wrist toward me. "If you bite me, will I change?"

I snorted, the sound escaping before I could stop it, and a rush of relief flooded through me. She was still here. She was still...herself. I shook my head, moving toward the far end of the kitchen where a sleek panel was set into the wall. I pressed my thumb against it, and the compartment clicked open, revealing what looked like a high-end wine fridge. Instead of vintage green bottles, it contained rows of blood bags.

Her gaze flicked from the bags to me. "Fancy. The bar could use one."

I grabbed one of the bags. "No, you wouldn't change," I said, and I moved to a personal sous vide machine—my preferred way to warm the bags without damaging the cells—setting the temperature to 98°. The machine hummed to life, and I leaned against the counter, glancing at Kit. "You have to completely die to be undead. Do you want me to tell you where I got them? The bags, I mean?"

Kit shook her head. "I don't see why it matters," she said. "I don't ask what farm my steak came from, and I don't see piles of dead bodies anywhere." She paused, a conflict battling on her lips over whether they would turn up in a smile or down in a frown. "Well, other than last night."

I laughed, a small, genuine laugh, and I could see the way Kit's shoulders relaxed at the sound. The sous vide machine beeped, and I pulled the bag out, pouring the blood into a posh black mug that I'd picked up in Paris some decades ago.

"Is it like in the movies?" she asked.

I looked into the mug, then back up at her. "Which ones? Some are far stupider than others."

That earned me the ghost of a smile. She said, "How hungry you get? That it becomes uncontrollable?"

It was a fair question. "If I exsanguinate a human completely, then I'm good for a little over a month. If I drain what I need but keep them alive, we have to refill more quickly. Blood donation rules. You know how you can only safely donate one pint, and then it takes a month and a half before you're back up to speed? We're losing cells at the same rate.

Our hunger tells us how close we are to weakening beyond the ability to hunt for ourselves. If we don't honor the thirst, natural selection takes over, and—" I snapped my fingers, "poof."

"And…drinking the blood of animals?"

"Please don't tell me you're talking about—"

"No!" She raised her hands. "I'm not about to ask if you're a fangless vegetarian sparkle vampire. But in a lot of the Dracula re-imaginings, they consume livestock in a pinch."

"In a pinch is right," I muttered. "Blood is not one for one. It's why they can't give you a pig's blood transfusion. Hit me with another."

"Okay," she said, drumming her fingers. "If you're real, what else is real?"

"All of it."

"All of it?"

"All of it."

She waited for me to expand. I did not.

"Do you want to talk about last night?" I asked, my voice gentle. I didn't want to push her, but I needed to know. Needed to know if she was okay, if she was still with me in all of this.

Kit chewed her lip. "Yes," she said, "but not right now." She looked up, a small, playful smile on her lips. "I need to shower, change, and get to work, or my boss will kill me."

I arched an eyebrow, my lips curling into a smile. "Yeah, I've heard that about her."

Kit's eyes twinkled when she smiled. She pushed away from the counter. "See you at the Page Turner," she said, and with that, she headed for my private elevator and disappeared, leaving me alone in the quiet kitchen.

I sipped the blood, wondering what farm this steak came from. I could taste the balance of vitamins and minerals in each serving, which usually gave me context clues for age, affluence, and sometimes gender of the blood donor. This one tasted like someone with a vegan diet, which I found endlessly amusing.

I looked at the place where Kit had been standing, remembering how she'd offered me her wrist. Had she meant it? Or was just trying to appease me because she was afraid?

I wandered through the penthouse, my fingers brushing against the edges of the furniture, the smooth surfaces of the artifacts I'd collected over the centuries. Antiquities, some of them priceless, others simply sentimental—a collection of moments from a life that had spanned far too long.

I paused in front of a painting, the colors vibrant even in the dim light. It was one of the few things I had left of Cetina. I reached out, my fingers grazing the edge of the frame, and I closed my eyes, letting the memories wash over me. Cetina had been fierce, unyielding, a force of nature that had swept me off my feet and changed everything I thought I knew about love. She was gone now, lost to time, but in Kit, I saw a spark of that same fire, that same resilience.

I smiled, my eyes still closed, and I wondered what Cetina would think of Kit. I bet they would be friends. They had the same spirit, the same stubbornness, the same refusal to back down, even in the face of danger.

I turned away from the painting, my gaze sweeping over the rest of the penthouse. The luxury, the opulence, it all felt hollow sometimes, like a cage I'd built for myself. But maybe it was big enough for two.

I finished the blood, set the mug down on the counter, and made my way to the bedroom to get ready for work. It was the day after the Cold Moon, after all, and I was on top of the world.

Dearest Cetina,

Something is happening to me.
   Something more than a crush.
   Something bigger than myself.
   Something, I think, you'd be happy for.

With love,
Yours

CHAPTER 8

ONE FOOT IN THE GRAVE

KIT

I tossed my keys onto the counter and made a beeline for the shower. I didn't want to be at Andy's place, but half my shit was here. It was my fault for leaving my makeup bag and black-on-black fits in his closet, but he lived so much closer to The Page Turner. It had made sense before I understood what a colossal piece of shit he was.

My hair was lathered and foamy when he walked into the bathroom without knocking.

"Where were you?" he asked, voice cold.

I spit the droplets soaking my face, rinsing my hair while ignoring him as best as I could. I couldn't believe he was starting shit now. He'd never asked me to stop escorting. He'd only mocked, belittled, and berated me until I stopped bringing it up. I hadn't done anything wrong. He knew what I did for a living. I was not responsible for what the client did after, or how Narya rescued me. I didn't ask to wake up on a wicked surgeon's table or be escorted through a sea of blood. I'd fallen asleep at a stranger's house, but he would, too, if he'd been through the night I had.

I rallied my courage. "Let's talk when I get out of the shower."

He reached in and turned off my water supply. "We'll talk now. You're cheating on me, aren't you?"

I glared at him, turning the water back on. "It's not cheating, Andy. It's work."

"Oh yeah?" He reached through the shower and grabbed my wrist. I yelped as he twisted it for me to see the bruises. "You got bruised from handcuffs at 'work?"

"Can you just let me get out of the shower first, for fuck's sake?"

I yanked my arm away and grabbed a towel, wrapping it hastily around my body as I stepped out of the shower.

Andy's eyes blazed, his hands balling into fists at his sides. "You're still doing it, aren't you?" he demanded. "You're fucking for money behind my back. I knew it. I fucking knew it."

I hesitated, my throat tightening. I couldn't tell him the truth. The truth was fucking insane. I couldn't explain that the bruises came from a crazed vampire surgeon, not some random client. I couldn't even explain why I'd kept escorting in the first place—not in a way he'd understand. He wouldn't hear anything but betrayal.

"I—" I started, but the words caught in my throat. I'd never intended to lie to him. I was as honest as he allowed me to be before the yelling started. I'd gotten smaller and smaller, only lying by omission while he told himself whatever assumptions made him comfortable.

"That's what I thought," Andy said, eyes glinting with something ugly. "Out there with your legs wide open for anyone who wants them, right? You're suppose to be my girlfriend, Kit. *Mine.* But you're for mother fucking sale to the highest bidder, probably catching AIDs and shit and then what, giving it to me?"

I felt something snap inside me, a surge of fury so intense it made my vision blur. "Fuck off, Andy. Are you fucking kidding me right now? You think I'm not safe? You think I don't get tested after every client? You think I didn't continue trying to talk to you every step of the way before you made this house terrifying?"

"I'm terrifying? *Me*? You know, I could have anyone I wanted. You think I don't have options? I have options. I'm in tech, Kit. You're a goddamn bartender hooker and I'm as close as you're ever going to get to happiness."

I turned off the water and stepped out of the shower, the towel barely clinging to me as I pushed past him, heading for the bedroom. "I'm done," I said, my voice shaking. "I'm fucking done."

I stormed through the house, grabbing my things, throwing them into my bag with a force that made the shelves rattle. My makeup, my clothes, a few small items I'd left here because, at one point, this had felt like home. During the sickly sweet, perfect months of love-bombing, *he* had felt like home.

Andy followed me, his voice a constant stream of accusations and insults, but I ignored him, my focus on getting out, on leaving this place behind. I yanked my outfits from the closet, shoving them into the bag and draping everything else over my arm, my hands trembling.

"Kit, you can't just walk away like this!" he shouted. "You owe me an explanation!"

I zipped up the bag, slinging it over my shoulder as I turned to face him one last time. "We're over, Andy," I said, my voice cold, final. "Don't contact me again."

I turned on my heel, my heart pounding as I made my way to the door. Andy's voice followed me, his final word boomed with anger.

"Whore!"

I didn't look back. I stepped out of the apartment, slamming the door behind me, the sound of it reverberating through the hallway. I stood there for a moment, my breath coming in ragged gasps, my hands shaking as I clutched the strap of my bag.

The tears came then, hot and unbidden. I could barely see as I made my way down the stairs, each step feeling like a weight lifting off my shoulders. I was done. Done with him, done with his anger, done with his accusations, done with his constant need to control me.

I ran through the night air to my car, chucked my shit into the back seat, and drove to the park to bawl my fucking eyes out.

I wasn't sad that it was over. I certainly wasn't sad to have him out of my life. But goddamn, I was despondent that I'd let myself be treated so poorly, that I'd been so in love with someone who looked at me like I was garbage.

Tears made an ineffective primer, but I did my makeup with shaky hands, combed my still-wet hair into a bun, and drove to the speakeasy.

With any other job, I would have called in sick to work after a shitshow like this.

But work meant Narya, and right now, she was the only person I wanted to see.

Chapter 9

Dearest (Vampire) Diary

Narya

The pen's rhythmic tapping was the only thing I could hear. My fingers moved without thought, a habit I'd picked up over the centuries—a small outlet for the restlessness that had taken root inside me. I tried to focus on the paperwork in front of me, the contracts and invoices that kept The Page Turner running smoothly, but goddammit if this girl hadn't made focusing impossible.

I wasn't usually one to let my emotions dictate my actions, but something about Kit had changed that. The idea of her out there, on her own, after everything that had happened...it made my skin crawl.

The security monitor on my desk flickered, and my heart skipped a beat when I saw her. Kit, stepping through the entrance, her eyes scanning the room as she shrugged off her coat. Relief washed over me, and I pushed my chair back, the pen falling forgotten to the desk as I hurried toward the speakeasy floor.

I was almost at the bar when the front door swung open again. Three sets of blue uniforms, shiny shoes, badges, and holsters with flashlights and handguns marred The Page Turner's upscale aesthetic. My steps faltered.

The conversation in the bar skidded to a halt as patrons went quiet.

One took the lead. "Narya Volkova? Seattle PD. We have a few questions for you about Colby LeBlanc."

My face was a mask of pretty neutrality. "I'm afraid that name doesn't ring a bell."

The lieutenant procured a picture.

"Oh, Cain? He took a security job for us not too long ago. He's late for work, in fact. You can talk to him when his shift starts."

I caught Kit's eyes and knew our shared secret was in safe hands. Besides, if the police got too wise on the subject, I had a few immutable tricks up my sleeve. They asked to speak to my staff, to which I of course complied.

"Jensen? Be a doll and tell our guests the distraction is almost over, and that we'll comp their last drink."

He looked between me and the cop, waiting for my signal that it was okay. At my subtle nod, he said, "You got it, boss."

I had nothing to be worried about. The police were safe in their ignorance: some douchey patron applied for a job, and I gave it to him. How were any of us to know he'd been using a pseudonym?

Kit didn't look up at me again. Her phone hadn't stopped buzzing since she arrived. Even now, as she silenced it, the screen continued to light in thirty-second intervals. Her face was paler than I'd ever seen. Her fingers flew over the screen. She looked...distressed. My gut twisted.

"No texting at work," I joked softly, if only to get her to look at me.

Her face twisted with fear and guilt as she met my eyes.

I made my way over to her, my hand brushing lightly

against her arm. "Are you okay?" I asked, scanning her face. I wished Hollywood hadn't been a sack of shitty liars when they'd claimed some vampires could mindread. Honestly, I'd love any of the witch powers that the movies insisted we had. It would make my afterlife much easier if those rumors were true. Unfortunately, I'd have to leave those abilities for other things that went bump in the night and settle for beauty, immortality, strength, wealth, and being hypnotically convincing.

Perhaps vampires didn't have it so bad.

She stared at me, lips parting in a wordless answer. Before she could say anything, one of the policemen turned, his gaze locking onto us.

"Kit, is it?" he asked. "Can we have a moment of your time?"

If I'd had a heart, it would have stopped. I didn't want her name in their mouths.

Kit looked at the officer numbly. She brushed passed me as she followed him, handing me her phone without a word.

I looked down at her phone, the glass rectangle still lit. Andy. A barrage of texts, one after another, his words vile, threatening. He'd told everyone. Friends, family. He'd even let the police know about her "little side hustle." I squeezed the phone so tightly that it nearly cracked in my palm. I turned my back on the police, as I was certain the adrenaline had triggered my fangs. I couldn't keep the rage to myself as I sneered at the screen.

I took a deep breath, locking the phone and slipping it into my pocket. I wasn't going to let this happen. Not here. Not now.

I turned, striding after the police, my heels clicking sharply against the polished floor. They were standing near the back, their voices low as they spoke to Kit, their expressions a mix of curiosity and suspicion. I didn't give them a chance to say anything else.

"Officers," I said, my voice cold, cutting through their

conversation. "While you are welcome to stay for a drink, you're ruining the night for my patrons. Please exit, and only return if you'd like a cocktail."

The lieutenant gave me a bored expression, if I could be bullied into compliance by some need to impress a man. "You know that won't reflect well on your establishment, ma'am."

"Neither does having you in my bar in uniform," I said, face sweet, words acidic. "At this stage, gentlemen, I'm afraid you've overstayed your welcome."

The policemen turned, their eyes narrowing as they took me in, but I didn't give them a chance to argue. I reached out, my hand closing gently but firmly around Kit's elbow, guiding her away from them.

"Jensen," I called over my shoulder, my voice sharp. "Ensure the officers make it safely to the curb."

"Yes, ma'am," the bartender replied, his voice steady, and I heard the soft murmur of the staff as they moved to comply.

I looped my fingertips into the crook of Kit's elbow and hurried her back to my office.

I started pacing. "I can handle the police," I said, my voice tight. "I've dealt with worse, and they don't scare me. But you..."

"What about me?" Kit took a half-step back. I recognized the fear on her face.

"Oh, shit, no. No. I'm not talking about…I'm not mad about *that*. Have you seen the girls who always sit at stools one and two? Do you think they're just very thirsty regulars?"

She blinked at me. "Well, no, I assumed they were working girls, but—"

I pressed my fingertips into my temples. "They're *my* working girls. They're safe as long as they're here instead of doing in-calls from home, or worse, doing out-calls at a client's residence." I couldn't look at her as I said this. "I have a past in this line of work, Kit. It's how I became the way I am, and it's one fucked up story."

"We…haven't discussed what happened the other night. The car…"

I nodded. "We haven't had a chance to talk. Everything happened so fast. You were nearly run down in the street. I took you to the Center, Seattle's vampire hub, after your concussion, but I didn't realize it was a full moon. We can get into it later, but we have something more time sensitive right now. Dangerous clients are trying to run you over, and if your asshole of an ex is to be believed, the police will be breathing down your neck any moment."

"The police wouldn't know shit if it weren't for my fucking ex and his fragile ego."

I hated what it said about my priorities that even now, in the midst of our troubles, I felt a squeeze of relief at the word 'ex'.

I couldn't look at her while I spit out the next few sentences out of my mouth. "I can't keep you safe when you're working from home. You need to be able to fight back. Against men, against the police, all of it. I—"

I was so distracted trying to spit out my garbled message that I barely noticed she crossed the room until she rested her hand on my arm.

"Narya," she said, "There's a solution."

My brow furrowed. She couldn't possibly be implying what I thought she was.

"Change me," she said. "Make me a vampire."

My jaw dropped. I didn't have the air required to make a joke about u-hauling. There was moving fast, and then there was a human choosing to end their mortal life after one sexless night together.

"You don't know what you're asking," I said.

"Yes, I do. You probably didn't grow up with vampire books and movies so you didn't get the chance to think it through before you were changed. This is the sort of hypothetical I've had a lifetime to figure out. I know my answer."

"You wouldn't be alive, Kit. Not anymore."

"My will to live has never been particularly strong," she said, joke dark, voice low. "Maybe my will to be undead will be stronger. What do I have to lose?"

My laugh was soft, almost noiseless. "Everything."

She shrugged. "And everything to gain."

"Being changed is…raw. It's the deepest connection two people can share. It's as intimate as sex. Maybe even moreso."

She chewed her lip. "Well in that case, it'd be a shame to choose between the two."

Dear Cetina,

I...I think I'm in love.

I really do think you'd be happy for me. But more importantly, I'm coming to see how happy I am for you. You didn't live hundreds of years to see your parents and siblings and their children die. You didn't watch kingdoms rise and fall, the maps change, the world goes from a burgeoning network of hope and education to the stupefied entertainment-hungry zombies who have ten thousand years of knowledge at their fingertips and the apathy to match. You were one of the first to die when that man entered our home, so you didn't know how much horror and darkness this world contained. You didn't have to live to see me become a monster.

But if you had...you would have seen me open up again. I'm not all the way there yet. I have a long way to go. But I'm willing to try. For her, I'm willing.

I will never stop loving you. Though I am nearly ready to let you go.

With love

CHAPTER 10

___

LOVE AT FIRST BITE

KIT

My heartbeat was so loud it was physically painful. I was positive Narya could hear it.

Her penthouse was so much clearer now that I wasn't passing out from the combination of shock and concussion. That fated night of carnage felt like a distant memory. She'd stood in the doorway, drenched in blood like the savior in a nightmare—the rescuer in a horror film. I was the final girl, and she…well, she was both the monster and the hero.

I hadn't realized that her penthouse was curved. The windows encircled the topmost floor, brushed concrete flooring, black silk sheets, bespoke cabinets and armoires curving with the windows, mounted art and antiquities like the most breathtaking private museum, items priced in the millions.

And then the most beautiful piece of art: her.

She was carved from marble, ice-gray eyes shone bright like diamonds, pale hair slicked into the same high-fashion ponytail she always wore. She tilted her head to the side, waiting.

"Are you sure you want this?" she asked.

"I've never been more certain," I said.

She unbuckled her black belt, tugging it slowly from the

pleated black pants. She unzipped them, then stepped out of them easily, still in her stilettos. Her silk top dropped to cover most of her panties, but saliva filled my mouth as I glanced at the silken bits just below the shirt's line. I felt like I'd die if I didn't taste her.

I wanted this more than air, so why was I so afraid? I'd read once that hunters tried to kill their prey quickly, as the cocktail of fear hormones ruined the meat. I wondered if the same was true of my blood—if I'd be acidic, somehow. Undesirable.

Narya took a step closer, sliding her cool hands over my hips. Fingertips brushed hair away from my face, then cupped my chin. My heart continued to thunder as she brought her mouth closer, making me incredibly aware of her fangs. Her full, crimson lips hovered above mine by scarcely an inch, and then she paused. I waited, and waited, and waited.

One of two things had to happen: either we'd kiss, or I'd go insane.

I grabbed her, slamming my body into hers as I closed the gap. I kissed her as hard as I could, lips moving in tandem, tongues a blur as we stumbled backward toward the bed. I'd thought I was pushing her, but the only thing leading the charge was my delusion. I'd forgotten how strong she was until she spun me in an instant, flipping me onto my back. I hit the mattress with a soft thump. She yanked my hips to the edge of the bed as she tugged off my pants.

"Wait, I haven't showered—"

"Shut the fuck up," she breathed. She kissed from my knee up my thigh, speaking between kisses. Her knees were on the floor beside the bed, fingers holding my hips. "I'll only stop if you don't want this."

I was going to have a heart attack.

I squirmed. "I'm queer, I swear, but I haven't been with a woman before. Not all the way, anyway. There was this girl in college who I...I might not be any good—I don't know what

I'm doing. I mean, I've been with women, but only as a provier, you know? In threesomes? Not as... I—"

"Then I'll teach you," she said, pausing right above my pussy.

She puffed a tantalizing breath through the thin fabric, drenching me. I wanted her mouth, I wanted her fingers, I wanted her tongue, I wanted *her*.

"Fuck, I'm wet," I moaned.

She tugged my panties over my knees and chuckled. "You're not just wet," she murmured.

I sat up, horrified. My fingers shot to my pussy and came up tinted with a light, brownish red. "Oh my god, I'm so sorry. Holy shit this is embarrassing. I didn't—"

Her fingertips dug into my hips, holding me in place. She arched a manicured brow. "Are you kidding me?"

"I..." It took ten heartbeats for my fog of humiliation and stupidity to pass. *Blood*. Of course. Still, it was a challenge for my brain to reconcile. "Are you sure?"

"Baby, this is my Christmas," she said. "Now lay the fuck down."

Her lips brushed over my pussy, gentle kisses, soft touches from an unflexed tongue as she warmed me up. Juices and blood flooded me, sticking to my inner thighs as I moaned, hips rolling. Her hands moved higher up, holding me firmly in place at the waist as my rhythmic grinding against her face moved me up and down off the bed. Her tongue began to move in consistent circles, applying more pressure as I gave myself over to her.

I screamed in pleasure when her fingers entered me. I'd been terrified of her razor-sharp nails, but I felt only the soft pads of her fingertips stroking in tandem within me. She began to suck my clit harder, draining me. I barely had the capacity for thought, though I managed a pleasant *fuck you* to men and their inadequacies.

My vision blurred. I gripped the sheets in both hands, unable to control the moans as they came quicker, faster, closer together. Her pumping matched the tempo of my groans, every suck, every lick, every stroke increasing with unbroken intensity.

"I'm—" I choked on the thought. *I'm in heaven. I'm going to die a perfect death. I'm totally and completely yours.* "I'm cumming," I managed.

It was as if a million fireworks exploding in each of my synapses, from the base of my spine to the tip of my toes. I'd never been so utterly enraptured, nor had I unraveled in such a whole, and perfect instant. It was a million birthdays, it was heroin, it was the very essence of both life and death themselves.

I lay there, a shell of a woman, only to look down at her as she cleaned the blood from her lips with a slow, seductive lick. She sucked her fingers clean like she had that night in her office. She maintained eye contact as she winked, then returned to my inner thigh and sunk her teeth into my artery. I gasped, but the pain and pleasure blurred together so inextricably that I could scarcely separate one from the other.

I had no idea how long she drank from me, only that the tingling lightheadedness of blood loss was the perfect companion to the dizzying drunkenness of a spectacular orgasm.

When she crawled up next to me, slipping her arm beneath my head and tucking me against her, I wondered if it was too soon to tell her that I was truly, madly, deeply in love.

CHAPTER 11

IT'S ONLY FOREVER

NARYA

We lay entwined in the afterglow, our bodies pressed close, the warmth of Kit's skin seeping into mine. The world felt small here, beneath the dim lights of my penthouse, with the city a blur beyond the windows. In this moment, it was just us—just the soft rise and fall of her breath, the gentle rhythm of her heart beneath my fingertips.

I was down bad, utterly obsessed with the softness of her skin, the hourglass curve where her waist dipped into her generous hips and ass, the way her sounds filled the room, whether laughter or glorious moans. I loved the way her eyes sparkled with that insatiable joy for living in the moment, her joie de vivre. I'd lived for centuries, seen more than most could ever imagine, but nothing compared to Kit. Nothing compared to the way she looked at me, like I was the reason for her happiness, like I was enough.

And then she said it.

"Do it," she whispered, her voice soft, her lips brushing against my ear. "I'm ready."

I froze, my fingers stilling on her back, my heart clenching in my chest. I'd known this moment was coming. But now that it was here, the weight of it pressed down on me, and I hesitated.

"This can't be undone," I practically whispered. "There's no going back, Kit."

She smiled, her eyes meeting mine, and she reached up, her fingers brushing the hair from my face, tucking it gently behind my ear. "Give me something to live for," she said, her voice so filled with conviction it nearly broke me.

My breath caught in my throat, my eyes searching hers. "You can live for me now," I said, my voice cracking. "As a human. You don't have to..." I trailed off, the words catching in my chest. But I could see it in her eyes—the determination, the fearlessness. She'd already made her choice, and there was no changing her mind.

The truth was, I understood. I understood her need for power, her need to be able to protect herself, to never be vulnerable again. I'd been there once, a long time ago, when I was young and fragile and lost. And I couldn't let what happened to Cetina happen to Kit. I wasn't strong enough to lose her too.

I swallowed, my chest tight, and I nodded. "You have to die," I said softly, the words almost too much to bear. If I could cry, I would. My eyes felt desperately dry, aching for release, but I knew that if I let myself cry, only blood would come out. I couldn't let her see that.

"And there's no one I'd rather have kill me," Kit said, her voice gentle, her lips curving into a soft smile as she leaned in, brushing a kiss against my lips. It was tender, filled with trust, and it nearly shattered me.

I cupped her face, my thumb brushing against her cheek as I looked into her eyes. "I love you," I whispered, my voice break-ing. I didn't give a shit if it had been three years, three months, or three days. This was my person, dead or alive. And then, before I could hesitate, before I could let my fear take hold, I leaned in, my lips pressing against her neck, my fangs grazing her skin.

I felt her shiver beneath me, her breath catching, and then I bit down, my fangs piercing her flesh, her blood flooding my senses. It was warm, rich, filled with everything that made Kit...Kit. Her laughter, her kindness, her fire. I drank, my heart breaking with every swallow, my tears mingling with her blood as I drained her, slowly, carefully, until her heartbeat began to falter.

I pulled back, my breath coming in ragged gasps, and I looked down at her, her face pale, her eyes fluttering closed. "I am so in love with you," I whispered again, my voice cracking, and I waited. Three minutes. I had to wait three minutes, until I was sure she was truly gone, until her human life had fully ended.

It was the longest three minutes of my life. I watched her, my hands trembling as I held her, her body limp in my arms. I counted every second, my heart pounding, and when the time had finally passed, I bit into my wrist, the blood flowing freely, and pressed it to her lips.

"Drink," I whispered, my voice breaking. "Please, Kit. Come back to me."

I held her, the seconds stretching into eternity, and slowly, slowly, I felt her begin to move. Her lips parted, her eyes fluttered, and she drank, the life flowing back into her, the transformation beginning. I held her, and I waited.

The transformation was agony. For both of us.

Kit screamed, her body convulsing as the last vestiges of her humanity burned away. Her veins filled with fire, her skin cold and clammy beneath my hands. I stayed by her side, my heart breaking with every cry, every plea. I wanted to take the pain from her, to bear it myself, but all I could do was hold her, whispering reassurances between her screams.

I answered calls between her cries, my voice steady as I spoke to Jensen, instructing him to manage the bar, to keep things running while I stayed here, with her. I couldn't leave her. Not now. Not ever.

The hours bled into days, the world outside fading away until it was just two of us in this small, dark room, the curtains drawn, the lights dim. I held her through every moment of it, my fingers brushing through her hair, my voice a constant murmur in the darkness.

And then, finally, it was over.

The room was quiet, save for the soft, steady rhythm of Kit's breathing. I looked down at her, her face pale, her eyes closed, her body still. She was drenched, damp hair clinging to slick skin, and I knew this would be the last time she would sweat—the last time she would shed the moisture of a human body.

I stroked the damp strands of her hair, my heart aching with relief, with love. "Good morning, Lazarus," I whispered, my voice soft, filled with awe. "How are you feeling?"

Kit opened her eyes, her gaze meeting mine, and I saw it: the change. The depth, the power, the hunger. She looked at me, her lips curving into a small, tired smile. "For the first time," she said, her voice barely more than a whisper, "I feel truly alive."

I let out a breath I hadn't realized I'd been holding, my chest tight, and I pulled her closer, pressing my lips against her forehead. She was here, and she was mine.

CHAPTER 12

TOMB IT MAY CONCERN

KIT

The days blended together, a whirlwind of new sensations, of power, of freedom. I felt like I was flying, my body no longer bound by the limitations of mortality. I was strong, I was powerful, and for the first time in my life, I was truly unbreakable. I wondered if becoming a vampire had truly made me more beautiful, or if it was the confidence dripping from every pore that gave me a renewed sense of just how hot I could be.

Narya and I spent our nights together—at work, at home, laughing at the movies or hunting in the shadows, shopping or slaughtering. The world was ours. Our colleagues at The Page Turner no longer whispered when they saw us touch or exchange glances. I moved into Narya's penthouse, my few possessions scattered across the space in a way that made it feel like mine too.

It was strange, in the best possible way. The life I led now seemed a thousand miles away from the one I'd had before. I loved the feeling of Narya beside me, the way her presence was constant, steady. I loved how easy everything seemed now that

I was no longer human—how the things that had once seemed impossible now felt like child's play.

I was in love, and I was ready to take on the world.

But of course, the world had a habit of sneaking up on you when you least expected it.

***

Two weeks into my new life, my phone buzzed with a message that pulled me out of the haze of happiness. It was from an old friend—someone who still hadn't caught on to the fact that I was a different person now. The message was short, direct, and left my chest tight with anger.

Andy is threatening to tell your parents you're an escort if you don't call him back. He's lost it. Are you okay?

I read the words over and over, my vision blurring with rage. The audacity. The absolute gall. He'd told my friends. He'd threatened the police. But my deeply religious family was the lowest blow I could fathom. Even now, after everything, he still thought he could control me, still thought he could hold something over my head. He couldn't accept that I was gone— that I had moved on. He still wanted to make my life hell, and he was willing to drag my family into it.

I clenched my phone, my new strength bending the metal slightly, and I took a deep breath, trying to steady myself. This had to end. And it had to end now.

***

The sleet hit the pavement that night in soft splatters, the sound barely audible as Narya and I stood outside Andy's building. I looked up at the windows, my heart thrumming with anticipation. The cold was nothing to me now—it barely registered.

I hit the buzzer, my finger steady, and waited for the static-ridden response.

"Yeah?" Andy's voice crackled through, the familiar sneer in his tone.

"It's me," I said, keeping my voice calm. "I'm here to talk."

There was a pause, and then a laugh, cold and mocking. "Oh, you're here to talk now? Finally ready to face me, huh?"

I forced myself to stay calm, to keep my voice even. "Just buzz me up, Andy."

Another pause, then a click, and the door unlocked with a buzz. I pushed it open, Narya following silently behind me as we made our way up the stairs.

Andy opened his apartment door, his eyes widening slightly when he saw that I hadn't come alone. His gaze flicked to Narya, confusion clear in his eyes, before he smirked, the expression as hateful as always.

"So, what's this?" he said, his voice dripping with disdain. "You're a dyke now? That's why you left me? Couldn't coax another cock into that diseased pussy so you found whatever chick would have you?"

I met his eyes, my lips curling into a smile that was anything but kind. "Right, that's how it works. You were such a pathetic excuse for a man that you turned me gay. Good job."

Andy's face twisted in anger, but I didn't give him time to respond. Narya and I stepped forward, slowly circling him, our movements deliberate. His bravado faded as his gaze flicked between us.

We circled until he was trapped between us, lionesses cornering their prey.

"Do you know what your problem is, Andy?" I said, voice low. "You think you can control people. You think you can manipulate them, love-bomb them, then trap them. But you can't. Not anymore. Not ever again."

Andy was too stupid to understand the sort of danger he was in. "What the hell are you talking about?"

"You'll never have the chance to be a controlling, manipulative, love-bombing narcissist to another woman again," I said. "You'll never have the chance to dox a sex worker again. This is the end of the line."

Andy stared at me, face reddening as anger—seemingly the only emotion he was capable of—flushed his features. His eyes darted to Narya, but she was practically serene as she awaited my lead.

Narya reached into her purse, pulling out a small photograph and holding it up. Andy's eyes flicked to it, confusion clear in his gaze.

"And it's such a shame you killed poor Colby LeBlanc," Narya said, her voice smooth, almost pitying. "You two went to university at the same time, right? Different fraternities? Some rivalries never die...but people do."

Andy blinked, his mouth opening and closing, the confusion deepening. "I don't—what—?"

Narya turned, slowly walking around the apartment, her movements graceful, unhurried. She began pulling items out of her purse—small things, personal things. Cain's things. She placed them carefully, deliberately, amidst Andy's belongings, wiping her prints away with a cloth.

She pulled out a vial, the dark liquid inside catching the light, and splashed it across the bathroom sink, the tiles. Cain's blood—the last human blood he'd had in his system before she'd made him hollow. She'd had centuries of practice and knew exactly what she was doing.

"Or were you lovers?" Narya asked, her voice thoughtful as she looked over her shoulder at Andy. "You've made enough homophobic comments tonight that I think it might be lovely to craft a legacy that you, yourself, were closeted. Is that how you'd like to be remembered?"

Andy's face twisted in fury, his eyes narrowing as he spat out, "As a motherfucking *queer*? Fuck no! Fuck you."

"Lovers it is," I said, nodding in agreement. I stepped closer, my eyes never leaving his. "And what, Colby wanted to go public, and you wanted to stay in the closet? So, you killed him for it. That's not very progressive of you, Andy."

"I don't know what you're—" Andy started, but before he could finish, I lunged, grabbing his wrists and twisting them behind his back, forcing him to his knees.

"You have to drain him right until the point of death," Narya said, her voice calm, guiding. "Then, before his final heartbeat, you fill him with your blood so you're the one in control. He'll be gone."

Andy thrashed. His curses filled the room, but he couldn't move—not against my strength, not anymore. I held him steady, and then I leaned in. The skin of his throat popped like a ripe peach beneath my fangs. His blood filled my mouth and I cherished the flavor knowing it would be the last time I'd taste him.

I drank, and drank, and Andy's struggles weakened, his heartbeat slowing, his breath coming in ragged gasps. I could feel the life draining from him, could feel the moment he was on the brink, the edge of death.

"Okay, that's enough," Narya said. "If you go any further, you'll kill him. Feeding him your blood after he's gone will only turn him."

I pulled back, wiping the blood from my mouth. "We can't have him living forever," I said, my voice cold. "Just long enough to die alone in prison."

She punctured my wrist with a bite, then helped force Andy to drink my contagion until it was my blood pumping through Andy's veins. We dragged him into the shower, his body limp, his eyes fluttering closed.

Narya knelt beside him, her hand resting on his forehead,

her expression softening for a moment. "By the time he's conscious," she said, her voice gentle, "he'll be an extension of you. A puppet."

I looked down at Andy, my heart pounding, the weight of everything settling over me. "The police will have their killer," I said, my voice steady. "And I'll have my justice."

Dear Journal—

It's been a minute.

I've been too busy to write. There's an irony in waiting to live until after you're dead, but I'm here for every minute of it.

I'm writing this to reflect on just how far I've come and how much I've grown, and I don't just mean the impressive new fangs. I guess I could have just broken up with Andy and left it at that, like a normal girl, but I'm not a normal girl. Not anymore. And what's more, I found someone to be un-normal with.

She's wild and amazing, and I'm totally and completely in love.

I guess...I guess it really does get better. Though, sometimes you have to make it get better.

Maybe that's the lesson here.

The parasites will keep draining you until the day you bite back.

Kit

CHAPTER 13

OVER MY DEAD BODY

NARYA

Infatuated sex. Vacation sex. Breakup sex. Makeup sex. Hate sex. Love sex. No-strings-attached sex.

A million other varieties, all with their own flavors, intensities, and emotions. None of them feel quite like "We just framed your shitty ex for murder while getting me off the hook for some frat loser's death, and are both escaping into the night like masterminds while he faces twenty-to-life" sex.

Framing and brainwashing a man three weeks after your lover's vampiric transformation is a fang-tastic bonding activity, if you have yet to try it. It took ninety days from Andy's arrest to his speedy conviction—guilty on all counts, based on his confession and all the corroborating evidence. A fundraiser for LGBTQ+ awareness was formed by an anonymous donor in Cain's memory—a legacy that Kit and I found both useful. It was also a fitting, secondary justice to the sort of men who would be throwing tantrums from hell that their Proud Boy cishet names were affiliated with the rainbow alphabet. No, sex didn't get sweeter than this.

We barely hit the top floor of our building before Kit was all over me. Her hands were in my hair. She shoved me into the elevator wall so hard we left a perfect crack in the mirror. We were a blur of clothes and hair and smeared lipstick as we crashed through priceless antiques and shoved our way to the bedroom. Our clothes were in tatters somewhere in the hall.

Everything that mattered was right here, right now.

Kit may have never been with a woman before me, but fuck if she wasn't a natural. Her learning curve was virtually non-existent. Once we had a single taste of each other, we were the only thing we wanted to do. I knew I'd never have a good day again without her taste on my tongue.

She'd maintained her perfect tan through the transformation. If anything, she was more golden than before, sparkling with a metallic sheen that was as indestructible as she was. My pale fingers contrasted beautifully against her as I gripped and scratched, unable to pierce her impenetrable skin. She was as voracious as I, and though I had centuries of strength on her, I savored the confidence with which she initiated sex and pushed me around. We were the most consensual of bullies in the bedroom, and it would never be enough.

We were a feral, insatiable mess.

It had taken her a little adjusting to get used to blood as the only thing vampires could secrete. If she'd been self-conscious about being on her period our first time together, she'd changed her tune when she could taste someone new between my legs every time I was wet, always mingled with the power-ful, immortal contagion unique to me. I said she tasted like sunset. She said I tasted like life.

Considering what we were, the terms felt interchangeable.

She got up on her knees, hiking one of my legs up as she licked her thumb and started rubbing my clit. Kit threw one leg over mine in a spider-like entanglement of legs, me on my back, her up straight.

"I didn't take you for such a scissorer," I smirked, reaching up to caress her breast. I rolled her nipple between my thumb and forefinger, loving the way she threw her head back, gasping whenever I stimulated her.

"Male porn directors took it from women," she said between gasps, pressing our bodies together. Red smeared on our southernmost lips, staining our inner thighs with the last person we'd consumed in a shadowed alley. "Justice for scissoring."

I grunted my agreement, too pussy-drunk to say something more intelligent as our clits rubbed together. I heard the hum of a vibrator before opening my eyes to see the companion she'd brought with her to the bedroom. I took the tiny bullet and held it at the place we connected while she continued to rock her hips back and forth. It was wet, sloppy, perfect, red, debaucherous ecstasy.

My body rolled, hips and shoulders coming off the bed as I worked with her rhythm. She rode me like her afterlife depended on it, gripping my knees tighter, clenching her teeth. God, she looked sexy with fangs. It was conceited as fuck, but I loved knowing that I'd done that to her. I was the cause of the razor-sharp man-killers that glistened in the dim lighting while she brought me to the edge of climax.

I grabbed her and flipped her onto her back with a firm *thud*. She fought me for the top spot, but I pinned her hands to the bed. "My turn," I purred into her ear, holding her down. Her struggle was part of our game, and I couldn't get enough.

"I was so close," she grunted in frustration.

I was strong enough to grip her wrists in one hand while I fetched the obsidian strap-on from the bedside table. "Good. Now, be a good girl and hold still for me."

I released her just long enough to slip into the strap-on, which was all the time she needed to wiggle out from beneath me. I adored her sense of confidence that she could wrestle me to my back. She was a fucking impeccable switch.She rolled onto her stomach as if to crawl away.

"Big mistake." I grinned. I grabbed her waist once more, jerking her to her knees. Her breasts pressed into the bed as I nudged the tip of the strap-on into her. She groaned as I entered her. "Hold on, baby girl. I'm about to fuck your brains out."

We came once. Twice. Six times that night.

———

Cetina,

This will be my last letter. I know you would understand. I know you've been waiting a long time for me to be happy.

I don't believe I'm damned. Not anymore.

I'll never forget you.

With joy,
Narya

"Hey," Kit's voice came over my shoulder. "What are you writing?"

For the briefest instant, I felt guilty, as if I'd betrayed her, somehow. Then I remembered who I was speaking to. I lifted the stack of papers.

"I...I was in love a long, long time ago. She died the night I was changed. I've written her thousands and thousands of letters over the years. This," I lifted the page slowly, showering her the short lines of neat penmanship, "was my last one."

Kit's smile was thoughtful. "Is she the one whose portrait hangs in the parlor?"

My answering smile was sad, but it no longer hurt. "Yes, it is."

"Will you tell me about her?"

I nearly cried, but those tears would have belonged to joy. "Yes. Yes, I will."

———

The months stretched into years, and the sex only got better, more creative, more depraved. When it was gentle, it was sweeter than the molasses my human mother had once poured over our sticky cakes. When it was rough, we fucked each other within an inch of our afterlives.

The decades became centuries.

The Page Turner in Seattle became Razor's Edge outside of Anchorage became World's End in Scotland. We were bartenders, club owners, Madames; protectors of the oldest professions—drinking and fucking—and for a thousand years more, we'll remain the sharpened fangs of justice for sex workers, and the last thing an abusive misogynist sees before he dies.

On our two-hundred and thirty-fifth anniversary, Kit asked me how I knew we'd be forever, and I told her the truth.

"Blood is thicker than water is a mistranslation. The saying used to be: the blood of the covenant is thicker than the water of the womb," I said. "Destiny is what you make it, and you and me, my love: we're forged in blood."

Notes on Sex Work & Queer Stories

There is no trigger warning for sex work, just as there are no trigger warnings for loan officers, real estate agents, veterinarians, or authors. Sex worker empowerment and destigmatization is an issue that is important to me and is prevalent in many of my works. If something about sex work causes you discomfort, my goal is not to make the environment more comfortable for you, but to encourage you to confront thoughts and feelings of whorephobia.

For more information, please read the lived experiences, articles, and input from sex workers themselves as they contribute to https://tryst.link/blog/tag/articles/ and other resources.

There are no trigger warnings for queer stories, and unless we begin putting in a trigger warning for straightness, there never will be.

Intentional Homage to the Following Vampire Stories in Pop Culture

Sheridan Le Fanu: *Carmilla*

Bram Stoker: *Dracula*

Charlaine Harris Schulz: *True Blood*

Stephanie Meyer: *Twilight*

Anne Rice: *Queen of the Damned*

Kevin Grevious, Wiseman, McBride: *Underworld*

Joss Whedon: *Buffy the Vampire Slayer*

Eric Kripke: *Supernatural*

Kevin Williamson and Julie Plec: *The Vampire Diaries*

Acknowledgments

This one's for Haley, Lindsey, Kelley, Allison, Bela, and Cera. Thank you for diving in fang-first with me on this trip through sapphic lore and insanity. So many of you jumped on the chaos train to help me get this short vampire story into the world by Halloween. I couldn't have done it without Helena, my barnacle friend and favorite artist, and the amazing Rachel, Zachary, and LBE for matching my freak.

About the Author

Piper CJ, author of the USA Today bisexual fantasy *series The Night and Its Moon* and *No Other Gods*, and New York Times bestselling series *Fern's School for Wayward Fae*, is a photographer, hobby linguist, and French fry enthusiast. She has an M.A. in Folklore and a B.A. in Broadcasting, which she used in her former life as a morning-show weather girl, hockey podcaster, and in audio documentary work. Now when she isn't playing with her dog, she's gaming, binging cartoons, dissecting fairy tales, or disappointing her parents.

Website: www.pipercj.com

instagram.com/pipercj
tiktok.com/@pipercj

Content & Trigger Warnings

Rampant misandry throughout, misogyny and sexual harassment (met with swift justice), attempted manslaughter (met with swift justice), emotional abuse (met with justice), death and dismemberment, mentions of kidnapping/hostage humans, attempted dubious consent, attempted ritualistic sacrifice, hypnosis, mind control, homophobia (met with justice), depression, brief/fleeting reference to suicidal ideation, blood, alcohol, sex, group sex, sexual blood play, use of language derogatory language and cursing.